Praise for Three Shots

"Sweet isn't the first word that often comes to mind when reading a ménage novella but that's exactly what you get with Three Shots. Don't get me wrong, this story is hot as hell with both M/M and M/M/F scenes but it's also sweet, funny, well it's just plain beautiful."

-Padme's Library Review Blog

This is super steamy. The sex is quite engaging and the characters are all likeable. Rachel is a strong woman which I love! This is 100% angst free. Seriously, it's a fun, relaxing, hot story that is just so welcoming. I smiled pretty much through the entire book.

-Diverse Reader

I absolutely loved this book!!! I feel it was a lot different from many ménage books because it was not just about hooking up for them the whole time they actually developed something that meant something. Don't get me wrong those two guys can melt just about anything, but then throw in Rachel and that is just the balance that they need to make the perfect trio!!!

-Kristian Erdmann

Three Shots

by
Brigham Vaughn

© Brigham Vaughn
ISBN-13: 978-1546540885
ISBN: 1546540881

Cover design by Brigham Vaughn
Book design and production by Brigham Vaughn
Editing by Sally Hopkinson
Cover Images: © konradbak
© Andriy Bezuglov
© Yordan Rusev

The author acknowledges the trademarked status and trademark owners of the following songs mentioned in this work of fiction:
Heart of Gold: Neil Young
I Put a Spell on You: Jay Hawkins
Sweet Jane: Lou Reed
I'm on Fire: Bruce Springsteen

Printed in the United States of America
First Printing: 2017

Published by Two Peninsulas Press

TWO PENINSULAS PRESS

Acknowledgements

This story has existed in many incarnations over the years. Originally, it was a short story about a M/M/F threesome. Later, I wrote about the guys' first meeting and the second night they were together. Eventually, I decided to turn it into one cohesive story, which I worked on for a while before abandoning it partially-finished.

A short while ago, I pulled it out on a whim and went through the story and realized it was nearly a complete novella. I changed it from first person to third, then expanded the end of the story at the suggestion of several of my betas.

Each version improved the story and I am so incredibly pleased with the final result. I couldn't have done it without the hard work of an entire team of people. I want to thank K. Evan Coles for her beta reading and Sally Hopkinson for her editing of the original version.

I also want to thank Helena Stone, Allison Hickman, P.R. Chase, and Reader70 for their excellent beta reading. And Sally Hopkinson for editing this story yet again.

Thank you to all of my fans who followed me from M/M romance into this foray in M/M/F erotic romance and welcome to my new readers. I couldn't do this without you!

Table of Contents

A First Taste:
Reeve

Strumming his guitar softly, Reeve Jenkins glanced over at the man who had just taken a seat at a table near the stage. Reeve observed him carefully as he tuned the Gibson 6-string. It was so automatic by now he could nearly do it in his sleep.

Reeve couldn't say exactly why he was so struck by the sight of the guy, but he couldn't look away. He was slouched in his seat, and he'd already polished off a bottle of beer and was quickly working his way through a second. His slumped posture, glowering expression, and pained eyes told Reeve he was an unhappy man.

Despite that, he was handsome, with shaggy blond hair drawn back at the nape of his neck and stubble highlighting a strong jaw and square chin. His shoulders were broad, and from what Reeve could see, his body was long and lean. He was dressed in a well-worn pair of jeans, boots, and a black, long-sleeve T-shirt that fit his body snugly. When he downed the rest of his second beer, his Adam's apple bobbed, and for a moment, Reeve could picture him swallowing Reeve's cock down until his lips were pressed right up to the base.

Reeve shifted on the stool, feeling his dick begin to press against the fly of his jeans. The man signaled for another beer, and his interaction with the waitress was cool and distant despite her attempt to flirt with him. Reeve couldn't decide if that was a good sign or not. *Gay or just in a shitty mood?* he wondered. Reeve wasn't sure how far he'd get; the guy hardly looked like he was eager for company. If Reeve hadn't been set to play soon, he would have already been at the guy's table, but performing should give Reeve a chance to suss him out a little better.

Done tuning, Reeve half-listened to the bar manager announce that the show was about to begin and looked out at the crowd. Aces was practically a dive bar, and the seats were only half-full. Reeve was a no-name singer and guitar player who picked up random shows. He wasn't trying to make a career of it, but he loved playing, and the occasional gigs were enough to satisfy his need to perform.

Lukewarm applause greeted him when the manager stepped aside.

Reeve adjusted the mic on the stand before speaking quietly. "I'm Reeve Jenkins, and my first song of the night is going to be 'Heart of Gold' by Neil Young."

The man he'd been eyeing earlier glanced up and met Reeve's gaze as he began to play. His stiff posture relaxed as Reeve strummed the familiar chords, and they exchanged glances throughout the set.

He really seemed to like the late 1960s and early 70s songs Reeve covered, and as Reeve transitioned from "I Put a Spell on You" to "Sweet Jane," the stranger leaned forward in his seat, watching more intently. Something passed between them, some connection, and Reeve suppressed a triumphant smile. Now, he was determined to talk to him after he was done performing.

Reeve's final song was by Bruce Springsteen, and he made sure to look right at the blond-haired man when he crooned the final lines. "Only you can cool my desire. Oh, oh, I'm on fire."

A smattering of enthusiastic applause wrapped up his set. Reeve stowed his guitar in its case, stashed it out of the way backstage, and walked out into the front of the bar.

A band was setting up as Reeve walked over to the man he'd had his eye on all night. He was nursing a bottle of beer—his third or fourth, Reeve wasn't sure which—and Reeve hoped the guy could handle it. He really didn't want to take home someone too drunk to do him any good. Reeve raised an eyebrow as he reached for the chairback, and the guy nodded once, slowly, his gaze never wavering.

Reeve slid into the chair and held out his hand. "Reeve Jenkins."

The guy chuckled but didn't reach over to shake. "I figured that out from your intro. Good show, man."

His speech was low and slow, with a seductive hint of a Southern drawl that had Reeve eager to hear him whisper dirty, dirty things in Reeve's ear as he fucked him from behind.

"Thanks." Reeve motioned for the waitress and ordered a beer. The as-yet-unnamed stranger shook his head when Reeve offered to buy him one.

"I'll take water, though."

"I'm glad you liked the set," Reeve said once the waitress was gone.

"I did. You've got a great voice." His posture still seemed wary, and his expression was neutral.

Reeve pressed. "I didn't catch your name."

He raised a single eyebrow and gave Reeve a crooked smirk that made dimples pop out on his cheeks. "Didn't give it, but you knew that. It's Grant. Grant McGuire."

"Very nice to meet you, Grant." Reeve held out his hand again, and this time Grant took it, his palm cool and damp from the bottle of beer, the back of his hand warm. His handshake was firm, and his skin felt good against Reeve's. It seemed like they were both a little reluctant to let go, so Reeve pressed on.

"Do you want to talk about it?"

"About your show? Sure. I liked the Van Morrison song you did. One of the best covers I've heard of 'Someone Like You'."

Reeve shook his head and leaned back in his seat, only half-aware of the waitress bringing their drinks. "Thanks." He nodded absently and took the bottle. "And, thank you, Grant. But I meant why you're morose and drowning your sorrows in umpteen bottles of Heineken tonight."

Grant raised an eyebrow again. "You sure don't mince words."

"Do you want me to?" Reeve asked, amused.

Grant shrugged. "I don't particularly need to spill my guts to a stranger tonight. If I had, I would have sat at the bar and unloaded on the bartender."

"Come on," Reeve coaxed. "What do you have to lose?"

"Fine. I ended a relationship."

"Shouldn't you be celebrating?"

Grant cracked a smile, but pain lurked behind his eyes. "I really loved her. But she needed something I couldn't give her. I ended it because I knew it was best in the long run, but it hurts like a son of a bitch."

"I'm sorry," Reeve said honestly. "But, at least, you ended it before it dragged out even longer."

"There is that."

"So, did you just come to this bar to drink away your troubles, or were you looking for something else?" Reeve asked, trying to get a feel for Grant. He had an ex-girlfriend, but given the way Grant had been looking at him during his set, there was definitely some attraction there. Hopefully bi then. And if Reeve was lucky, looking to get laid tonight.

Grant shrugged. "Mostly the drinks; although, I was glad to see they had some musicians playing tonight. I was surprised when I heard you sing. You're better than I expected."

Reeve gave him an amused grin. "Thanks, I think."

"Naw, you know how it is. Half the people who play in places like this can't carry a tune to save their life."

"True," Reeve agreed, taking another drink of his beer.

"You do this for a living?" Grant asked.

"Nope. This is just for fun. Actually, my brother and I own a music shop over on First Street."

"Huh, you live here? I figured you were from out of town or something," he said.

"Yeah, grew up here. You?"

Grant shrugged. "Moved here for college. My family is originally from down south."

"So I gathered from the accent."

He chuckled and drained his water. "There's no hidin' that, I suppose."

"I wouldn't want you to," Reeve said flirtatiously. "In fact, I can think of a few things I'd really like to hear you say."

Grant quirked the eyebrow again. "What are they?"

"Words definitely not suited for polite company."

Grant glanced around and shook his head. "I wouldn't call the crowd here at this bar polite company."

The crowd wasn't too rough, but it wasn't a gay bar either. Not unfriendly, but not exactly friendly either.

Reeve shrugged and decided to lay it all out there. "Well, definitely not the kind of crowd who wants to hear two men talking dirty to each other either."

Grant smirked. "Where did you have in mind?"

"My place. How about you come home with me and let me see if I can make you forget all about your recent breakup?"

"I'm not sure I'd be very good company tonight."

"Let me be the judge of that."

"You're persistent, aren't you?" he asked wryly.

Reeve gave Grant his most charming grin. "I try."

Grant stood abruptly and nodded toward the door. "What the hell. Why not?"

Reeve stood, too, but a bit more slowly. "Now if that isn't the least enthusiastic response to asking someone to come home with me I've ever gotten, I don't know what is."

Grant grimaced. "Sorry, I'm rusty at this. I don't remember all the dance steps."

Reeve grinned. "I'm pretty good at dancing; I'll be happy to show you all moves you've forgotten. And maybe a few you've never tried."

Grant stepped closer, his expression lightening. "You think you can teach me something new, huh?"

"Maybe. Even if I can't, it'll be fun trying," Reeve said huskily.

The corners of Grant's lips curled up in a grin, and his eyes brightened. "You have that right."

Up close, Reeve could smell the subtle allure of his cologne. It made Reeve want to bury his mouth right up against Grant's neck and twist his fingers into his hair. He settled for slowly wetting his lips with his tongue. Grant's gaze followed his every movement. When his breath stuttered, Reeve suppressed a grin then stepped back. "Let me get my guitar, and we can head out."

Grant nodded, something a little dazed and surprised in his eyes, and turned to the bar as Reeve hurried backstage. Clearly, there was attraction there, but Reeve was still half-afraid that when he returned Grant would be gone.

But he found Grant leaning against the bar, elbows planted firmly on the scarred top, and a booted foot drawn up on the rung. The way he stood stretched the material of his shirt across his pecs, and Reeve had the urge to press his palms to them and feel the hard planes of his muscles.

Reeve sauntered over to him, letting his walk become a looser-hipped swagger. "You ready?"

"Mhhhmm." One corner of Grant's mouth turned up in a smirk. "I think I am."

They went through the usual talk of assessing each other's sexual health as they walked out into the parking lot. It saved them an awkward conversation in bed later, and Reeve was grateful he was fully stocked with condoms and lube; nothing killed the mood like running out mid-fuck.

He gave Grant his address so he could follow Reeve to his apartment. It was nothing special, just a decent place he'd lived in for about a year. Mostly, he liked not having to deal with the bullshit of roommates on the rare occasion he took someone home.

Reeve pulled into his designated spot as Grant parked a few rows down. Grant followed him into the building, up the stairs, and then into his place. Reeve heard the door click shut behind him as he walked into the living room, tossing his keys and wallet onto the coffee table in a habit so ingrained he didn't think twice.

Reeve turned to Grant. "Want a beer?"

He shook his head and stalked toward Reeve. There was something predatory in his walk and gaze that made Reeve's stomach tighten and his cock twitch. Grant didn't stop until he was pressed right up against Reeve, one hand on his back and the other cradling the back of his head. His lips were soft but eager, and Reeve closed his eyes, glad to see he'd lost whatever reluctance he'd felt before. Grant didn't hesitate to slide his tongue into Reeve's mouth, tasting faintly of beer and the cigarette he'd smoked on the way over.

Reeve's hand tangled in Grant's hair, deepening the kiss. He wrapped a hand around Grant's hip and tugged him close. His body was all hard, long lines, taut muscle, and easy grace, and Reeve was dying to learn the way he'd move against him. Top or bottom, Reeve didn't really care, he just wanted to get Grant in his bed.

The kiss was deep, and Grant made a low, throaty sound when their hips met and cocks brushed through the layers of fabric. Reeve kept their lips connected as he moved his hands up under Grant's shirt, his skin hot and smooth. Skimming the shirt up over his chest, Reeve grazed his nipple with the side of his hand. Grant let out a strangled gasp of pleasure and ground their hips together. Reeve tore his lips away so he could pull Grant's shirt off. He raised his arms to help, his gaze glittering hungrily as he reached for the flannel Reeve wore. He shrugged it off and felt Grant's fingers at the hem of his T-shirt. They worked together to get it over his head so it could join their other clothes on the floor.

The moment it was off, their lips were on each other again, eager and rough. This time, the kiss was harder, more frantic. Reeve backed up toward the

14

couch until it hit the backs of his knees and fell onto it, one finger in the waistband of Grant's jeans, tugging him down. More controlled, he lowered himself, their booted feet tangling together as their hips met and their bare torsos pressed together. Grant's skin had a light, golden tone, and it felt scorching hot against Reeve's. The rough, deep kisses continued as he ground down, the pressure making Reeve's cock weep and an ache build in his balls.

Fuck, it had been too goddamn long since he'd been with someone. With Grant tugging at his hair and leaving wet kisses on his jaw, Reeve could hardly think straight enough to remember who it was he'd been with last. *A woman,* he thought hazily. *Violet, maybe?* That triggered a memory. Yep, crazy redhead—explosive in bed, but a little too clingy out of it. Reeve ended things after a few times together. His cock had missed her, but the rest of him sure hadn't.

"What are you thinking about?" Grant asked roughly, the vibrations of his voice against Reeve's throat sending another wave of lust through him.

"Trying to remember the last time I got laid," Reeve said a little breathlessly, pressing a hand to the nice swell of Grant's backside, forcing their hips together. He let out a groan at the increased pressure on his dick.

"And?" Grant prompted, his teeth grazing Reeve's Adam's apple. He swallowed convulsively.

"Too fucking long ago. In fact, if you're not careful, I'm going to come in my fucking pants." Reeve groaned again and shifted. He was way too close to the edge.

Grant immediately pulled back, reaching for Reeve's belt buckle. "I'd rather you come in my mouth." He made quick work of it, and without removing the belt, unbuttoned the fly of Reeve's jeans. Reeve raised his hips, and Grant hooked his thumbs into the waistband of his boxers then pushed downward, but everything got tangled up when he reached his ankles.

"Shit, wait." Reeve sat up and chuckled as he sat back. "Fucking boots," he grumbled as he hastily untied the laces and yanked one off his foot.

Grant did the same with his own boots, and Reeve was amused to realize that their choice of footwear was keeping him from having Grant's lips around his cock. *Damn it.* He couldn't stop the chuckle that escaped his lips. Grant looked over and grinned. It was the first true amusement Reeve had

15

seen on his face, and they laughed at the absurdity. The mood went from charged to something lighter, more relaxed. A sense of camaraderie suffused the air as they both finally got their boots off, and they looked at each other again.

They reached for each other simultaneously, and Reeve found himself pressed to the cool, smooth leather of the couch. Grant hovered over him and closed a hand around Reeve's length. The low, rumbling groan that left his chest grew louder as Grant began to stroke. Reeve loved pussy—the taste of it, the way it felt to be inside of it, but no woman gave a hand job quite like a man did. The larger hand, the firmer grip, the way a guy knew precisely where to focus the attention; they all combined to make a very pleasurable experience. And despite the lack of lube, Grant's touch felt incredibly good.

"Thought you wanted me to come in your mouth," Reeve said roughly.

Grant smirked. "Oh, I do."

"Then you better get your fucking mouth on my cock because I'm way too close," Reeve growled.

Grant released him and kicked off the clothes still bunched around his ankles as he slid down the couch and settled with his head between Reeve's thighs, propped up on one elbow. Reeve widened his legs, drawing one knee up so his foot rested flat against the couch. Grant began with Reeve's balls, his fingers hot as he gently cupped and rolled them in his palm.

"Christ," Reeve groaned, his eyes clenching tightly closed as he reveled in the feeling. Grant's teeth grazed his inner thigh, and Reeve felt Grant's hot breath ghost across his cock before he swallowed. He didn't deep-throat Reeve, but it was damned close, and the feel of his dick suddenly engulfed in the shockingly warm wetness sent a shudder through his body.

"Jesus fucking *Christ*," Reeve gasped when Grant began to slide his mouth up and down. He moved smoothly, easily; his mouth sucking, his tongue flicking and tapping, his hand on Reeve's balls, tugging and rolling them expertly. Reeve slammed one hand down on the cushion of the couch and buried the other in Grant's soft hair.

Reeve's entire body was rigid with tension, strung so tight he felt like he'd splinter into a million little pieces; needing, wanting. He could hear the wet sounds of Grant sucking his cock, felt the way his tongue cradled it, and the

16

rough ridges along the roof of his mouth as the head of it slid in and out. Reeve's body burned for his release. He felt it everywhere: in his fingertips, in his toes, but nowhere more strongly than at the base of his dick. It was agonizing and perfect, and when Grant swallowed, increasing the suction, it roared through Reeve. It incinerated him, burned away everything but the pleasure. Time seemed to slow. He could focus on nothing but the feel and sights and sounds of Grant swallowing.

There was a roaring in Reeve's head, and his mouth fell open, a hoarse, agonized sound reverberating in his throat. "Fucking *hell.*"

Time sped back up, and he became aware that he gripped Grant's hair tightly. He loosened his hold, stroking the soft strands in gratitude as he lifted off. Grant made one last slow, sweet stroke up the shaft of his cock, curling over the head before letting him go with a press of his lips to the tip.

"Jesus, Grant. That was the best fucking head I've ever gotten." Reeve's body still trembled, every muscle gradually loosening as the tension seeped out of him.

Grant sat back, a smug little smirk playing across his face. "And here I was thinking you were supposed to be teaching me some new moves. Seems to me like it's reversed."

Reeve sat up, bracing his arms on the couch. "I suggest we move this to the bedroom then because it's about time I deliver on my promise."

L ocked together, hands roaming and lips meeting, they stumbled through the apartment. Grant gripped his bare ass and ground against Reeve as they passed the kitchen. Reeve lurched over to the table, bending Grant backward over it as he ravaged his mouth. When the pressure of his renewed erection was too much to handle, he tore his mouth away and stepped back. He stripped Grant out of his jeans and boxers before pushing him down into a chair.

Reeve knelt on the floor at Grant's feet and nipped at his inner thighs, grazing them with his teeth, teasing Grant the way he'd teased Reeve. Burying his nose against the crease of Grant's leg, Reeve inhaled the faint, musky scent of his skin mingling with the clean smell of soap. His mouth moved to Grant's sac, placing soft, wet kisses across it. He heard Grant moan lowly and glanced up to see his head fall back as Reeve gripped his dick. Reeve made a few slow, experimental strokes with his hand, and Grant's thighs tensed. They were close in size, although the head of his cock flared wider, and Reeve shivered with anticipation at the thought of Grant pushing inside him.

Reeve sat up, stretching to reach Grant's chest as he continued to stroke with his right hand. He brushed his left thumb over one nipple while his mouth descended on the other. Grant's cock twitched in Reeve's hand, and his chest rumbled with a groan as Reeve continued. Grant panted and squirmed in the chair by the time he switched sides. Reeve was still on his knees, stretched out over him, and stroking him became awkward with the limited space between their bodies.

Reeve lowered his head until it was level with Grant's cock again. He opened his mouth and dropped down, taking Grant in as far as he could before drawing back to tease the head with his tongue. Grant was sprawled in the chair, his hands gripping the edge of the seat. Reeve watched the corded muscles of Grant's thighs and the lean definition in his stomach as his body tensed. Grant threaded a hand through his hair, encouraging him, and Reeve closed his eyes, allowing Grant to guide him. He wasn't rough, using just enough pressure to set the pace, and Grant moaned when Reeve took him a little deeper. Loving the way he responded, Reeve eagerly continued until Grant urged him to lift. Reeve sat back, wiping his lips on the back of his hand.

"Bedroom?" he asked quizzically.

Their gazes locked, and Grant's expression made Reeve shiver with anticipation. "No. Kitchen table. I wanna fuck you, *now*."

Reeve hurriedly got to his feet and had hardly straightened before Grant spun him and bent him over the table, running a hand down his spine. Reeve moaned when he felt Grant's cock graze his ass cheek.

"Where are the condoms and lube?" he asked roughly. "I can't wait any longer."

"Over there," Reeve pointed across the kitchen. "Top drawer."

Grant strode over and yanked it open, fishing out condom and lube before slamming the drawer closed with a solid thud. He swiped a towel from the counter and walked over to the table. "You're going to have to tell me why you keep them in here."

18

Reeve grinned and twisted his head to watch Grant. "It's a long story."

"After, then." Grant ripped open the condom wrapper and deftly sheathed himself.

Reeve heard the sound of the bottle opening, and in a moment, he felt a cool, wet finger slide between his cheeks. Reeve widened his stance. Although, Reeve suspected Grant was as eager as he was, Grant took a moment to slide his finger across Reeve's entrance, moving over it teasingly before applying gentle pressure. He pushed the finger in a little way, giving Reeve's body a moment to acclimate before sinking in all the way. Reeve moaned and dropped his head to where his hands rested on the table, arching his back so Grant could prepare him more easily.

Grant fucked him with one finger, moving methodically until Reeve squirmed and panted.

"Ready for two?" he asked roughly.

"Please," Reeve pleaded.

Grant withdrew from his body briefly, then two fingers pushed in, slick with fresh lube. Reeve breathed into the stretch, and in a few moments, Grant could easily slide both fingers in and out. He twisted his fingers inside Reeve with every in stroke.

The pressure was amazing, and Reeve felt sweat break out on his forehead.

"I'm good. I want your dick in me," he begged.

"Thank fucking God," Grant muttered. He slid his fingers out, and Reeve glanced over his shoulder. Grant quickly wiped his fingers clean with the towel and settled behind Reeve, his hand warm on Reeve's hip as he aligned himself. He pushed in slowly, allowing Reeve time to accommodate, but the moment Reeve relaxed and pushed back, he began to move. Grant's cock felt better than Reeve had dared imagine, and the fluid rhythm of his hips made Reeve moan.

"Christ that's good," Grant groaned. "Goddamn."

"I know," Reeve panted. "Harder."

Grant pounded into Reeve, who heard the screech of the table as it slid across the tile. "So fuckin' tight," Grant moaned.

Resting his forehead against the table, Reeve reached his arms wide, his hands gripping the edges on each side so he could get better leverage. It bit into Reeve's stomach, but he didn't care, too caught up in the way Grant fucked him to worry about it. Reeve's cock throbbed as one particularly deep thrust grazed over his prostate. "Fuck," Reeve cried out.

He heard Grant fumble with something before he hauled Reeve upright, one arm wrapping around his chest, the other gripping his dick. Grant's hand was slick with lube, and Reeve heard the bottle fall to the floor as he was bent over the table again. Grant used the arm around Reeve's torso for leverage, and he slid his hand over Reeve's cock. The quick rhythm Grant set, coupled with the deep fucking, made Reeve's eyes roll back in his head.

"I'm gonna come soon," Grant ground out between clenched teeth. "Are you gonna shoot for me, Reeve?"

Reeve's palm slammed down onto the table, scrabbling for the edge again as he pushed back. "I'm close."

With a harsh, rough cry, Reeve came just a few strokes later, feeling like his body was being turned inside out as he erupted all over the table. Pleasure burned through him, white-hot and electric. His ass clenched around Grant's cock, and Grant grunted, his face buried against Reeve's back, his breath hot against Reeve's bare skin. After a few erratic jerks against Reeve's ass, he stilled, panting.

"Holy fuck."

After a few long moments, Grant straightened and gently withdrew. Reeve winced—it had been a while, and they had gotten pretty rough at the end—but it wasn't anything he couldn't handle. Grant dropped onto the chair beside the table, but Reeve stayed bent over, arms braced on the table, panting.

After a moment, Grant chuckled lazily. "You were right; you did show me a few new tricks."

"Oh, yeah?" Reeve turned his head to look at him, his body still trembling a little.

"Never fucked anyone over a kitchen table before. And I can't think of the last time I came that hard."

Reeve grinned and stood, exhausted and exhilarated all at once. "Glad to hear it."

There were two bathrooms in the apartment, so clean up took no time at all, and Reeve was spraying down the kitchen table with disinfectant when Grant came out of the guest bath. They were both dressed again, and Grant jammed his hands in his pockets and leaned against the counter. "Want some help with that?"

"Nah, I'm good. Thanks, though."

"Sure." Grant watched him clean for a moment, and the silence was surprisingly comfortable. It was interrupted by the growl of his stomach, and Reeve glanced over at him in surprise. Grant sheepishly grinned. "Apparently, I worked up an appetite."

"Hmm, I probably have stuff for sandwiches; you want to stay and eat?"

Grant thought for a moment, then nodded. "Sure. Sounds good."

"If you want to poke around in the fridge while I finish cleaning up, that's fine," Reeve offered.

Grant sauntered over to the fridge and rummaged around in it for a moment before lifting his head. "Hmm, have any tomatoes?"

"Yep, there are a couple on the counter over there." Reeve gestured toward them, and Grant glanced at him.

"BLTs good?"

"Sounds fantastic."

Reeve gave the table a final wipe-down, then washed his hands and worked with Grant to make the sandwiches. Grant cooked the bacon while Reeve washed the lettuce and sliced bread and tomatoes.

"Toasted?" Reeve asked, holding up a piece of bread.

Grant gave him a look of surprise. "Of course."

Reeve shrugged. "Just checking. People can be pretty particular about things like that."

Grant gave him a dimpled grin. "Fair enough. I'd throw a fit if it wasn't toasted."

When the sandwiches were finished, they sat at the table with their BLTs, a bag of barbecue chips unearthed from the cupboard, and some bottles of root beer.

Grant took a huge bite of his sandwich and chewed, moaning appreciatively at the taste. He washed it down with a sip of his soda and spoke. "So, I really am dyin' to know. Why the condoms and lube in the kitchen drawer?"

Reeve snorted and set down his food. "It was dumb, honestly. My ex and I were constantly going at it all over the apartment. She got fed up with me running to the bedroom every time, so I made some joke about stashing them in the 'junk' drawer."

"Junk drawer." Grant laughed heartily and shook his head, amusement crinkling the corners of his eyes. Reeve snickered and shrugged. Another glance at Grant had both of them chuckling, and in no time, they were both laughing loudly together.

Reeve shook his head once their laughing fit ended. "I know. But the name kind of stuck. And that actually was a good spot for them." He shrugged. "The girl and I split up, but I kept stashing them there."

Grant nodded, a smile still playing at his lips. "So I take it this isn't the first time you've used the kitchen table."

"No, although, it's the first time I've ever been bent over it. Usually, I'm the one doing the bending."

"I have to admit I'm curious," Grant admitted, idly spinning his beer bottle. "So you're a switch *and* bisexual?"

"Yep. I like to keep things fluid."

"Really?" Grant said. "That's interesting. I don't meet many men who are."

"Yeah, I haven't met many who are either," Reeve mused, licking a smear of mayonnaise off his thumb.

"I am, too, actually," Grant offered. "I just wasn't really feeling like bottoming tonight."

"Huh. Well, tonight was great," Reeve said with a shrug. "It's been a long while since I've been thoroughly fucked."

Grant gave him a slow grin. "Happy to oblige."

They sat around talking for another hour or so, digging into the stash of chocolate chip cookies Reeve's mother had dropped off a few days before. They discussed music for at least half the time, eventually venturing into the topic of jobs. Reeve owned a shop that sold musical instruments, and Grant worked for a construction company doing computer modeling. He didn't offer much besides that, steering the conversation away from very personal subjects, and Reeve didn't push him. Their banter was lighthearted, and they laughed a lot. Grant's hazel eyes shone when he was enthusiastic about something, and he had a habit of pushing his hair behind his ear when he talked.

When the last of the cookies had been devoured, Grant stretched and stood. "I should probably head out."

"Okay," Reeve said. He stood and walked Grant to the door. Grant stopped and turned to face him.

"Tonight was exactly what I needed. Thanks, Reeve." His smile was heart-stopping.

"You're welcome. I'll be playing at Aces again. I'm usually there the first Thursday of every month. Stop by if you'd like a repeat."

It had been a great night; the sex and the conversation were both fantastic. Grant had just gotten out of a relationship, though, and Reeve was in no hurry to get into one. Leaving things open-ended seemed like the best approach.

Grant smiled, and Reeve wondered if it was just his imagination that Grant seemed relieved. "I might do that."

They kissed goodbye—a long, full-body kiss that was equally a hello and a goodbye.

"See ya around, man," Grant said as he stepped through the door.

"See you around, Grant."

Whistling, Reeve closed the door behind him and walked into the kitchen to put away the dishes. His time with Grant tonight had been just right. He had a full belly and a sated cock.

What more could a man need?

A Second Shot:

Grant

Grant shifted the beer bottle back and forth between his hands, his skin prickling with anticipation. Earlier tonight when a group of friends asked him where he wanted to go for drinks, he mentioned Aces, the dive bar Reeve played in.

The night he met Reeve wasn't something he could easily forget; great sex and interesting conversation rarely went hand in hand, and he had offered both. Grant had been meaning to go back to Aces on the first Thursday of the month and see if Reeve wanted to hook up again, but he hadn't gotten around to it. So when friends suggested going out to hear music, and he realized Reeve might be playing that night, he made sure they ended up at Aces.

Grant hadn't caught a glimpse of him yet, though, and he was getting antsy. "What's up with you tonight, Grant?" Ryan asked.

He shrugged and drained the remainder of his beer. "Nothing. I'll be back."

Ryan nodded and Grant walked over to the bar, propping his booted foot on the rung.

The bar was pretty packed, the bartender scrambling to keep up with demand, and Grant waited patiently to order another Heineken. When he did, the man nodded at him and turned away. Just a moment later, Grant felt a warm hand on his lower back.

"Glad to see you here, Grant."

Startled, he turned around, smiling when he saw Reeve standing there. "Hey, I was starting to wonder if you were playing tonight."

"Came here to see me, huh?" he asked smugly.

25

Grant chuckled. If there was one thing he liked about Reeve—apart from his gorgeous good looks—it was his confidence. He had both in spades. He was tall and lean, with thick brown hair, chiseled cheekbones, and a lower lip that made Grant want to bite it.

Grant leaned back against the bar and smirked at him. "Yeah, I came with friends to see you play."

Reeve leaned in closer until Grant could feel the heat of his breath against his ear and down the side of his throat. "You didn't come to play *with* me?"

"Maybe a little of that, too," Grant admitted, knowing he wasn't referring to music at all. Good thing since Grant had zero musical talent. Just an appreciation for hot guitarists like Reeve.

Reeve gave him a slow smile. "Glad to hear it."

A slightly annoyed voice caught Grant's attention. "Sir?"

He turned to see the bartender waiting with his beer. "Shit, sorry."

Grant reached for his wallet but Reeve shook his head and leaned in to talk to the bartender. "Hey, this one's on me, okay, Stu?"

"Sure thing, Reeve," the man said.

"Thanks." Grant grabbed his beer, and Reeve followed him as he stepped away from the bar. "It's crowded tonight," he commented.

"It is, and I'm not sure why."

"Maybe there are a lot of people here who heard about the hot guitar player who was going to be on tonight," Grant drawled.

Reeve snorted and rolled his eyes. "Yeah, the guy going on after me *is* pretty hot."

"Hmm, I'll have to keep an eye out," Grant joked. "Maybe I'll go home with him instead."

Reeve laughed. "And maybe I already have someone to take home, so I won't care."

"You couldn't handle two?" Grant teased, taking a sip of his beer.

Leaning against the wall, Reeve chuckled. "You know I could. I was just teasing, though."

"Yeah, I know." Grant gave him a speculative look. "Still, it's something to consider."

"You'd be up for that sometime?" Reeve asked, interest lighting his eyes.

"Sure."

"Male or female?"

Grant shrugged. "Either is fine. I think finding someone who we both agree on, and who wants both of us, will be the difficult part."

Reeve gave him a slow smirk. "The first part, maybe, but the second ... I think you're underestimating how hot we both are."

Grant chuckled and took another sip of his beer, liking the way Reeve made him laugh, liking the way he made the blood in his veins heat. "Fair point."

"Either way," Reeve said. "I think I'd like it to be just the two of us tonight, if that's all right with you. We still have plenty to explore."

"That's more than all right," Grant said huskily.

Reeve leaned in. "How out are you to your friends?"

"Out enough. They've never seen me with a guy, but they know I'm bi," Grant said. "Why?"

"'Cause I want to kiss you right now."

"I'd be more concerned about them," Grant said, gesturing to the nearby table full of men giving them wary looks that bordered on the edge of hostile.

"Shit," Reeve muttered. "I forgot where we were. Come with me for a sec?"

"Sure," Grant agreed, setting his half-finished beer on a table covered with empties.

Grant caught a glimpse of Angela, a work friend, as he followed Reeve, laughing as she gave him a big thumbs up.

"What are you laughing about?" Reeve asked. "I think my ass looks pretty damn good in these jeans."

Grant explained what Angela had done and added, "Trust me, your ass looks great in those jeans," which made Reeve snicker.

They rounded the corner, heading toward the back of the bar. Reeve slipped through an unmarked door and took Grant's hand, tugging him in after.

The area where Reeve had brought him was a dim, crowded space behind the stage. There were chairs and various tables stacked along the back wall. Heavy, black curtains divided the area they were in from the performance space, and Reeve led him to a little nook on the far side, hidden by the chairs and curtains. He didn't waste any time, pushing Grant back against the wall, his lips hungrily devouring Grant's. Reeve's mouth was minty and warm, and his lips felt as good as Grant remembered from the last time.

Something about being with Reeve felt easy and uncomplicated. The attraction was there in spades, but Grant didn't feel the nervous tingle and flush of a new relationship. He didn't feel on edge, like he might get his heart broken.

Grant grabbed the belt loops on Reeve's jeans, tugging him closer. He was half-hard, and Grant slid his hand between their bodies to stroke him over the top of his clothes. He grunted and tore his mouth away, his lips moving to Grant's neck. Grant squirmed when Reeve found the sensitive spot below his ear, and he spun them around, crushing Reeve back against the wall.

"Wait," Reeve said hoarsely, and Grant backed off a little, thinking maybe he didn't want to continue, but he surprised Grant by dropping to his knees.

Grant braced himself against the wall the moment Reeve's hands went to his zipper. Grant was hard, and he groaned when Reeve's warm hands wrapped around his dick. Reeve's mouth was on Grant's cock before he could blink, hot and wet and so damn good. Last time, he'd been in charge, but now, he happily let Reeve lead.

Grant lowered one hand to cup Reeve's jaw, watching his cock slide in and out of Reeve's mouth. Reeve closed his eyes, concentrating, and Grant ran his thumb across his cheek. Fuck, he was pretty. Not feminine looking, but the contrast between his high, high cheekbones, long lashes, and square jaw gave him a ruggedly beautiful look.

"Fuck," Grant said with a quiet moan, and Reeve looked up at him through the lashes he'd just been admiring. Grant put a hand on the back of Reeve's head, winding his fingers through the thick, soft strands of his hair.

Reeve shifted a little, placing his palms against Grant's thighs and opened his mouth wider. Grant tentatively thrust forward, trying to feel him out; half-afraid he was reading Reeve's signals wrong. But the look in his eyes encouraged Grant, and he began to thrust slowly and shallowly.

The feel of his mouth on Grant's dick was amazing enough, but to let Grant fuck his mouth … Jesus, he could hardly take it.

Grant groaned as he sped up, Reeve's mouth giving him just the right amount of suction and friction. Reeve easily breathed through his nose, and with his hands on Grant's thighs, Reeve could take back control any time he wanted. It took away Grant's fear of fucking Reeve's mouth harder than he could handle and allowed Grant to relax. If need be, Reeve could stop him.

"So good, Reeve," Grant said through gritted teeth. "So fucking good."

His hand squeezed Grant's thigh in acknowledgement, and Grant hissed as he pushed a little deeper on the next thrust, the head of his cock bumping the back of Reeve's throat. Grant closed his eyes, trusting that Reeve could handle this. His fingers tightened on Reeve's hair as he felt the tingle in his body settle low in his belly. Grant tensed, his short, choppy breathing sounding loud in the quiet, dim space. He could hear the sounds of the bar—laughter and chatter mingling with music—but it was still quiet enough that he could hear the slick sucking sounds Reeve's mouth made when he thrust in and out.

"Close," Grant warned him, his jaw clenching, trying to delay the inevitable. Grant wanted to come, but this felt so good that a part of him didn't want it to ever end. "Your mouth is …" Grant groaned, his head falling forward as he braced one hand on the wall and the other on the back of Reeve's head as he continued to fuck Reeve's mouth.

One minute, Grant was barreling toward climax, and the next, he was there, spilling down Reeve's throat in desperate, hard spurts. Grant lifted his hand from Reeve's head and braced both arms against the wall. His head swam, and he felt his knees go a little weak. Reeve seemed in no hurry to let him go, slowly, torturously cleaning Grant up, paying particular attention to the ridge along the head of his cock. When he couldn't take another second, Grant let out a low groan and pulled away. The cooler air was shocking after the warmth of Reeve's mouth. Grant's hands shook as he tucked himself away and fastened his pants.

Reeve stood fluidly, and Grant grabbed him and pulled him in for a kiss. The taste of his come on Reeve's tongue made Grant's spent cock twitch, and it wasn't until Reeve's phone vibrated in his pocket that they finally pulled apart.

Reeve drew back with a sigh. He glanced at his phone and winced. "Shit, my set is about to start. Come home with me after?"

"Definitely." Grant smiled and leaned in to whisper in his ear. "It's so fucking hot knowing you're going to be on stage with my come in your mouth."

Reeve chuckled and captured his lips in a quick, deep kiss. He slid a hand to Grant's ass, squeezing lightly before letting go. "If you're up for it, I really want to fuck you tonight."

Grant let out a low groan, opening his mouth to answer, but Reeve was gone, disappearing around the corner of the curtains with a swagger to his walk. *Cocky fucker.* Grant liked that about him, though. Some men just knew how to pull off that kind of confidence without being an asshole.

Grant left more slowly, making his way back to the front of the bar. Angela raised an eyebrow at him when he slid into the chair beside her. "And who was *that?*"

"Reeve Jenkins," Grant said, his tone nonchalant.

She rolled her eyes at his less than informative answer and pushed up the sleeves on her shirt, revealing two arms covered in swirling, colorful ink. "Who is Reeve Jenkins?"

Grant was aware of the other eyes at the table, his co-workers' curiosity unmistakable. They knew he dated men and women—although, they'd never

30

met anyone but his ex-girlfriend April—and Grant was usually tight-lipped about his personal life. "Just this guy I met a couple months ago."

"He's fucking delicious," Angela said, taking a swig of her beer. "Tell me you've tapped that."

Grant chuckled. "We hooked up before, yeah."

He heard the announcement that Reeve was about to start playing and angled his body to see the stage better. Reeve's gaze met Grant's as he introduced himself and the song he was about to play. He lowered his head to look at the guitar resting on his lap but glanced up from under his lashes and licked his lips before he began. A jolt of arousal slammed into Grant, and he gripped the table, knowing Reeve had teased him intentionally.

It had worked, too. He shifted uncomfortably in his chair.

"And are you going to tell me what you two got up to earlier?" Angela asked quietly.

"Nope," Grant answered, his gaze never leaving the stage.

"Damn it," she grumbled. Her boyfriend was in the military and overseas. Grant had a feeling she was hoping to live vicariously through him. Grant wasn't embarrassed about what he and Reeve had done, but he disliked talking about his personal life with anyone.

Angela settled back with her drink, muttering curses at him, and Grant tuned her out to focus on Reeve again. He went through a number of covers of late 60's and 70's songs, singing in his low, husky voice. By the time his set finished, Grant was more than ready to go.

As quickly as possible, Grant said goodbye to his co-workers, found Reeve, and followed him to his apartment.

"Think we can make it to the bedroom this time?" Reeve teased once they were inside, tossing his keys, wallet, and phone on the coffee table.

Grant chuckled, remembering their impatience before. "I think we can manage it as long as we keep our hands off each other until we get there."

Reeve tilted his head toward the bedroom. "Get your fine ass in there then."

"Just my ass?" Grant teased.

"Mmmm, no, I think I'd like to play with the rest of you as well." Reeve gave Grant a broad, flirty grin. It *did* seem like play to Reeve. Not that it wasn't hot—hell, it was some of the hottest sex Grant had ever had with someone he wasn't in a relationship with. But more than that, sex with Reeve was *fun*.

Grant had been with both men and women who took it all so damn seriously, always wanting to be on their game, performing almost. Peter, a guy he'd dated last year, had been very concerned about the way he came across, hating when Grant saw him at anything less than his best, which put quite a damper on any emotional intimacy.

This genuine, easy connection with Reeve was so refreshing.

Reeve murmured directions to get to his bedroom, and Grant ventured down the hall, feeling the heat of Reeve's body against his back, although, Reeve never touched him.

Reeve's bedroom was as comfortable and relaxed as the man himself, with a large bed and several dressers. Grant dropped his keys onto one of them as he looked around. There was nothing showy about the room, everything had clean lines and soft, warm colors, and it looked like the kind of place a man could sleep easy in.

Grant felt the brush of Reeve's clothing, and the heat from his body settled against his back. He dropped his hands to Grant's hips, and his breath brushed Grant's cheek as he leaned in. "I've been thinking about this all night."

Christ Reeve was good at that. A few words and a couple simple touches and Grant was already hardening in his jeans. "Yeah. Me too."

Reeve slipped his hands under Grant's shirt, his palms warm on Grant's skin. Grant let out the breath it felt like he'd been holding since he pulled up at the bar earlier that night. His relationship with April had fucked with his head, and the thought of another serious relationship was daunting to him. Grant had considered one-night stands but the detached connection didn't appeal either. Reeve was warm, easy. Grant could sink into him for a night but walk away with his heart unscathed later.

"I need this," Grant quietly admitted, closing his eyes as Reeve's arm slid up, palm pressing against his sternum. Grant winced, hating how needy and pathetic he sounded, but Reeve merely pressed a kiss to the side of his neck and stepped back.

Reeve's gaze wasn't judgmental when he turned Grant to face him but warm. He didn't say anything, just slid his hands under Grant's shirt and lifted it off, removing his own before stepping closer. They kissed, bare chests pressed against each other and jean-clad legs twining together. Reeve was lean and strong, his skin pale and smooth under Grant's hand.

"I want my mouth all over your body," Reeve murmured, deftly unbuttoning and unzipping Grant's jeans, shoving them to the floor. Grant kicked off his shoes and socks—feeling rather smart for not wearing his boots like last time—then dropped his boxers, so he stood fully naked in front of Reeve.

Reeve's gaze was appreciative as he looked over at Grant, and the left side of his mouth lifted into a little smirk. "Mmm, yes. *All* over."

Grant's indrawn breath was a little ragged as he watched Reeve strip off his own clothing. He was gentle but firm as he pushed Grant onto the bed, and Grant settled there, waiting for his next move. "Scoot back," he coaxed, and Grant did, watching as Reeve dropped to his knees on the carpet.

Reeve ran his hands up Grant's thighs, making his cock twitch in anticipation as Reeve's head lowered. His lips were warm against the hollow beside Grant's hipbone, and he moaned when Reeve licked the spot.

"Shouldn't it be your turn?" Grant asked breathlessly, not really wanting him to stop. "After you blew me so spectacularly backstage …"

Reeve laughed, then trailed his tongue toward Grant cock. He looked up at Grant. "Oh, I'm not going to suck your cock right now."

Reeve's mouth returned to Grant's skin, and he felt the sharp little nip of his teeth on the sensitive skin right around the base of his cock. The sting melted into pleasure immediately as Reeve lapped at it with his tongue. Grant squirmed on the bed, his cock hard and beginning to leak at the tip.

"What the fuck are you going to do then?"

Reeve blew a cool stream of air across Grant's dick, and he shuddered, his hips bucking forward, his body desperate for more. "You just lay back and let me show you."

"Fuuuuuck," Grant whined.

But despite Grant's pleading, Reeve continued licking and nipping and sucking at the skin along Grant's hips and around his cock, even giving his thighs attention. Grant went out of his mind. No one had ever, *ever*, focused so much on his pleasure, and Reeve was clearly in no hurry. Grant felt torn, desperately wanting more stimulation but absolutely drugged on the feeling of someone taking their time to work him up like that. He couldn't stop squirming, especially as Reeve got closer and closer to his balls. And then, suddenly, one was in Reeve's mouth, which felt shockingly hot on the highly sensitive flesh there.

"Hnnngh," Grant ground out between gritted teeth and gripped the sheets below him in his fists. He shuddered when Reeve's tongue stroked his testicle, then let it slide from his mouth, immediately sucking the other one in. It was such a goddamn strange feeling to have his nuts in someone's mouth, but Jesus, if it didn't feel amazing.

"Don't stop," Grant begged, lifting his head to look down the length of his body at the man between his thighs. "Please, don't fucking stop."

Reeve glanced up, blue eyes mischievous and amused. Grant didn't know Reeve well, but the look told him Reeve planned to keep torturing him. Grant let his head fall back on the bed as Reeve continued.

After a few minutes, Reeve gently released him and slid his hands up Grant's thighs, pressing them up and back so Grant was open to him.

Grant felt a strange tremor of nerves twist his belly, eager anticipation warring with uncertainty. He was pretty damn sure he knew what Reeve intended to do, but Grant had never been on this end of the act. He wanted it—God, the way his cock throbbed and leaked, Grant knew he wanted it *bad*—but it still made him anxious.

Reeve's warm breath hit the sensitive skin between Grant's balls and ass, and Grant twisted on the bed, a shockingly needy whine leaving his lips.

"Has anyone ever rimmed you?" Reeve's voice was low and raspy, and the intensity of his gaze as he looked at Grant just increased his eager anticipation.

"No."

"Do you want me to?" Reeve asked. "If you don't, just say the word and I'll stop."

"Christ, Reeve. Do it, *please*," Grant pleaded.

Reeve lowered his head, and the first light, teasing touch of his tongue made Grant gasp. Reeve tormented Grant with darting, barely there touches at first, but when the flat of his tongue made a slow, deliberate swipe across the most sensitive part of Grant, he bowed up off the bed. "Holy fuck," he gasped.

Grant closed his eyes, screwing them tightly shut as he panted, body writhing under Reeve's sensual assault. "What the fuck are you doing to me, man?" Grant asked.

Grant felt the vibration of Reeve's chuckle against his skin, but his tongue didn't let up, and it made Grant's cock throb more. Grant reached up and grasped it, fingers gripping tightly as he jerked himself. Reeve alternated tormenting little teasing movements with long, slow, firm licks. Grant was flushed and panting, writhing on the bed trying to get as much friction as possible.

Grant groaned with disappointment when Reeve lifted his head. "Don't stop. Why the fuck are you stopping?"

"Are you okay with bottoming this time?" Reeve asked with a chuckle, his thumb grazing the sensitive skin he'd just been teasing with his tongue earlier. When he pressed his thumb forward, pushing just inside, the muscles in Grant's stomach clenched.

Grant blinked at him dazedly, trying to gather his wits. "If you keep licking and touching me like that, I'll probably agree to anything," he said breathlessly.

Reeve laughed against his thigh. "Good to know."

Reeve pulled his thumb away and resumed licking. His tongue curled and pressed inside Grant a little. Just enough to tease and make him want more. All Grant could focus on was the man between his legs and his goddamn magical tongue.

"Yes, fuck. Oh please, Reeve." Grant heard himself beg. "I'm not going to last much longer. I want you to fuck me."

With one last slow, teasing lick, Reeve pulled back with a grin and helped Grant lower his legs to the bed again. "Told you last time I'd show you something new."

"Jesus, you weren't kidding," Grant admitted. "Now, hurry up, goddamn it."

Reeve lifted his hand from Grant's leg, and a moment later, he heard the sound of a drawer opening and items shifting inside it. A few moments later, a cool, slick finger replaced Reeve's mouth and circled Grant's entrance. Grant's breath hitched, and he tensed momentarily, but Reeve just kept circling, teasing Grant until he pushed against his finger. Reeve shifted to kneel on the mattress beside Grant's hip, his lips hovering over Grant's.

Grant didn't think twice about kissing him, his mouth rough and hungry as he tried to thank Reeve for the pleasure.

Grant reached for Reeve's cock. It was so hard. Pre-come leaked from the tip, and Grant swiped his thumb across it. "Mmm, can't wait to feel this in me."

Reeve groaned and removed his finger, quickly reaching for the lube. As Grant slowly jacked Reeve's cock, Reeve prepared him with slick fingers. They were both panting by the time Grant was open and relaxed, ready to take him.

With quick, sure movements, Reeve covered his dick with a condom, He flipped Grant onto his stomach. Grant went willingly, feeling Reeve's warm body against his own. "I've wanted to do this since the first time I saw you," Reeve said, teasingly letting his cock slide between Grant's cheeks, the excess lube slicking the way. Grant shuddered with anticipation, so, so ready.

"Fuck me, Reeve," Grant said, his voice rough and eager.

He tensed for just a moment as the head of Reeve's cock nudged at his entrance, but Reeve's lips on the back of his neck distracted him. Lazy little kisses and nips from Reeve's teeth on Grant's neck were enough to help him relax, and as soon as he did, Reeve slid inside with a low groan. Grant winced when Reeve was fully seated; it had been a long time, and the man wasn't exactly lacking in the size department.

"How does that feel?" Reeve asked.

"Good," Grant managed, pushing back against Reeve as he began a slow, steady rhythm. It was so different from the last time, not frantic or hurried. Reeve took his time; although, there was nothing hesitant about his movements. There were no sweet words or romantic touches; this wasn't Reeve making love to him, but it *was* intense. Reeve clasped their hands together and pressed them hard into the mattress as he fucked Grant, the length of their bodies remaining in contact. The heat from Reeve's body and the controlled roll of his hips made Grant bury his face against the sheets and moan.

The slight burn and discomfort had faded, and in its place was a shivery sort of pleasure that raced up Grant's spine from where Reeve was buried inside him and spread out over his whole body. Reeve let go of his hands and snaked his arm underneath Grant, hooking his hands on Grant's shoulder for more leverage. Grant moaned when Reeve's cock brushed the spot inside him that made his eyes roll back in his head. Reeve chuckled when Grant bucked under him.

They shifted to their knees, and Grant grabbed onto the headboard, gripping it as if his life depended on it. There was only a brief hitch in Reeve's rhythm, then he was fucking Grant again, wringing sounds out of him that Grant had never heard himself make before. Once again, Reeve found his prostate, only this time the angle made Reeve nail it even harder. Grant began to shake, flushing at the incredible pleasure that was making him come unhinged.

Grant's hand flew to his cock, and the feeling of his fist closing around the sensitive head nearly sent him over the edge. "I don't know how much longer I can last," he ground out from between gritted teeth.

"Don't care," Reeve said hoarsely. With one firm hand on Grant's hip and the other curled around the top of Grant's shoulder, Reeve yanked him back so they were both upright on their knees. Grant cried out, jerking himself off furiously, not stopping when he came, spurting all over his hand and the bed. With a few more deep, hard thrusts Reeve joined him, grunting "Grant" into his ear. They were both panting as he sat back, resting his ass on his heels as he guided Grant down with him. Grant felt Reeve's temple press against the back of his head, and the warmth of his breath against Grant's sweaty neck.

Neither of them spoke for a long moment, sated and too damn comfortable to do anything but gasp for breath. Grant wasn't really sure what to say. His head was a bit fuzzy and muddled from the orgasm, and Reeve's arms locked around him were probably the only thing keeping him upright. It wasn't until Grant felt a cramp in the back of his thigh that he realized he had to move. He jerked away from Reeve, gasping as Reeve's cock disappeared from his ass. Grant fell onto his side, wincing in pain.

"What's wrong?" Reeve asked worriedly.

"Muscle cramp," he said between gritted teeth.

Reeve chuckled and shifted on the bed, moving his hands to Grant's thigh to work the muscle loose. Under his strong, kneading touch, the muscles eventually unclenched, and Grant was able to relax. He let out a relieved sigh, his body going slack.

"Better?"

"Much; thank you," Grant said sincerely.

Reeve let go with a pat to his thigh and got up off the bed, disappearing into the bathroom. When he returned, the condom was gone, and he had a warm, damp cloth to clean Grant and the bed. Grant didn't argue, feeling too wrung-out to move a muscle. Reeve discarded the washcloth on the carpet when he was done and collapsed onto the bed beside Grant, their shoulders touching as they sprawled diagonally across the big bed.

"Fuck, that was good," Grant said with a grin, turning to face him.

Reeve stretched lazily. "Yeah, it was. Think you'd like to do it again?"

"Have sex?" Grant raised an eyebrow at him in question.

"Bottom."

"Yep." Grant sighed and sat up, resting his arms on his drawn-up knees. "It's been a long time since I've been with a guy I'd let top me, but this was great."

Reeve chuckled, his hand coming to rest on Grant's back, fingers lazily trailing up and down his spine. "I get it. I liked fucking you, but if you'd rather top more often, I can live with that."

"Nah. This was good. Just what I needed." Grant relaxed, letting thoughts of previous partners drift away as he turned to look at the man whose bed he was in.

"Me, too." Their gazes met, Reeve's expression relaxed and content. "C'mere."

Reeve pulled Grant to him, and he went willingly. His mouth was on Grant's immediately, warm and undemanding. It was a thank you kiss, and Grant smiled against his mouth, realizing he could already tell the difference in Reeve's kisses. They kissed lazily for a long time, tangled in the mess of sheets, Grant's thigh thrown over Reeve's, Grant's chest half on top of his. Reeve made long sweeping strokes up and down Grant's back while he tangled his hands in Reeve's unruly hair and simply let himself enjoy.

Reeve began a slow, rocking rhythm against Grant, and he quickly realized they were both growing hard again. Grant glanced down at him, quirking an eyebrow in question. Reeve nodded, and it wasn't until Grant sat back and had the condom on his cock that he realized neither of them had spoken aloud.

How in the hell is it so easy to be with this man? Grant wondered. He was so good at keeping things contained that it wasn't until that moment Grant realized exactly how much he really had needed a night like this. Reeve's touch was comforting without being intrusive. He allowed Grant to feel like he could be himself without worry about censure or disapproval.

"You okay?" Reeve frowned up at him, and Grant realized he'd paused with his dick in his hand.

Grant smiled reassuringly at him. "I am. I'm just thinking how good this is. How easy. I don't get it."

Reeve shrugged. "I don't quite get it either, but I'm not about to look a gift horse in the mouth. Get down here and fuck me, Grant. For no other reason than we both want it, and we know it'll be damn good."

Grant smiled widely and slicked his fingers. "That's a good enough reason."

"Then stop over-thinking things," Reeve coaxed. "Just enjoy this."

Reeve pulled his knees up so his feet were flat on the mattress. Grant certainly didn't need any further invitation, and he reached forward, letting his slick fingers graze Reeve's balls then trail below to his entrance. To his surprise, there was already something there. Grant sat back and looked at him, finally noticing the base of a toy there. "What's this?" he asked teasingly. "Aren't you a dirty one? Did you have this in all night?"

"Mmmhmm." Reeve smiled smugly.

"Damn, that's hot," Grant hissed. His slippery fingers made the toy difficult to grasp, but he gripped it the best he could and gently twisted. Reeve drew in a sharp breath, closing his eyes. When Grant tapped on it, Reeve clamped his eyes shut tighter, his hard cock bobbing at the teasing torture. Grant slowly began to work it in and out of him, teasing him.

"Fuuuuuck," Reeve whined. His fists clenched the sheets, and his whole body trembled. If Grant wasn't careful, he was going to make Reeve come before he even got inside him. Grant gently fucked Reeve with the plug, coaxing him with his voice. "Are you ready, Reeve? Can I take this out and slide into you?"

"Fuck. *Please*," he said hoarsely.

With a few more slow, twisting slides, Grant withdrew the toy from Reeve's body. He let out a long, shuddering gasp, and Grant set the toy on the nightstand. It wasn't insubstantial in size, and Grant felt rather impressed. He'd never really had much occasion to use plugs like that, but he imagined it had been torturing Reeve all night.

"Ready for me?" Grant asked, lowering his body over Reeve's. The head of Reeve's leaking cock grazed Grant's stomach, and his hips bucked up as if seeking the pressure and friction. Grant shifted a little, allowing his cock to nudge Reeve's entrance. He widened his legs a little, and his hands grasped Grant's ass, encouraging him to move. Grant pressed into him; the toy had relaxed him enough that it was an easy slide in, and Grant let out a low, rumbling groan when he was all the way in.

"How does that feel?" he teased. "Better than the toy?"

"So much better." Reeve moaned, his blunt nails digging into Grant's ass. Grant stretched forward, kissing Reeve as he began to move. Foreplay and orgasms out of the way, this was fucking. Not rough exactly, but not messing around either. Grant had come twice that night, so he could relax and focus on something other than the urgent need to get off.

Sweat slicked their chests as Grant fucked him, paying attention to the way Reeve's body responded. His signals weren't hard to discern. When Grant moved in a way Reeve liked, his fingertips bit into Grant's skin, his jaw tightened, and he clenched around Grant's cock. Grant shifted and moved his mouth to Reeve's ear, speaking in a low, husky voice, letting the drawl become more pronounced. "You like that, don't ya, Reeve? Like the way I fuck you; like my dick inside you."

"Fuck, yes," he gasped.

"Mmm, I thought so."

Grant pushed up, bracing himself on his hands and knees so he could fuck Reeve slower and harder. His breathing picked up, and his hand moved to his cock. "Uh uh, I wanna see if I can make you come without you jerking off," Grant said roughly, and Reeve's hand fell to his stomach. "I want to see if I can make you come just … like … this."

Grant punctuated each word with a swivel and thrust of his hips. Reeve dug his hands into the sheets again, gripping them tightly. His clenched jaw and the way he shuddered under Grant led Grant to believe Reeve was close. Grant closed his eyes, focusing on using the roll of his hips to bring Reeve maximum pleasure. Just a few moments later, Reeve let go with a hoarse cry, come spattering both their bodies as he clenched around Grant's dick.

Grant let out a gasp, the rhythmic way Reeve's body milked his cock sending him over the edge. He bit back a howl, the overwhelming pleasure making his final thrusts short and erratic. Grant shuddered through the last of his orgasm, dropping down onto Reeve's chest to bring their mouths together. Grant kissed him hard, nipping Reeve's lips with his teeth. He tangled a hand in Grant's hair and forced their mouths apart. Grant looked down at him questioningly, and Reeve grinned.

"I was getting a bit lightheaded there."

Grant curled his lips in a slow smile and propped himself up on one elbow. "We have some really spectacular sex together, don't we?"

41

Reeve chuckled. "That we do."

They eventually dragged themselves out of bed, rinsing off in the shower together, mostly keeping their hands to themselves, but occasionally reaching out with a wandering hand or coming together for a brief kiss.

After the shower, they returned to the bedroom. Grant grabbed his jeans from the floor, fishing his phone out of the front pocket. "Hey, gimme me your number."

Reeve rattled it off, and Grant entered it into his phone, sending Reeve a quick text so he'd have Grant's number. "This way we can actually get together on purpose," Grant explained, "and not have it be hit or miss if I can make it to the bar on a night you play."

"Sounds great," Reeve said with a grin. Grant slipped on his boxers then his jeans.

"I'm not looking for anything serious, though," he warned Reeve as he buttoned them, not wanting there to be any confusion.

Reeve shrugged and lay back on the bed, naked, with his hands forming a pillow for his head. "That's fine. I'm low-key, Grant. Call me if you get horny. Hell, call me if you just want to go grab a drink. I have no expectations about where this will go. It doesn't have to *go* anywhere. But having a friend I can hop into bed with occasionally sounds great to me."

"That sounds perfect," Grant said, Reeve's easy-going ways relaxing him. He leaned down to kiss Reeve, bracing a hand on the bed beside him. Reeve broke away after a moment, grinning up at Grant.

"You better stop, or I won't let you leave," he said teasingly.

"Good point." Grant gave him one last kiss and stood, tugging on the rest of his clothes. He grabbed his keys off the dresser where he'd dropped them earlier, and smiled down at Reeve. "Want me to lock up on the way out?"

"That would be great. Thanks, Grant."

"I'll give you a call, okay?"

Reeve's eyes looked heavy-lidded and sleepy. "I look forward to it."

"And who knows," Grant teased, "maybe we'll find someone to join us one of these times."

Reeve stretched languidly with a low groan. "Mmm, I like that idea."

Grant left Reeve's place, his body content and his mind surprisingly calm.

Last Call:
Rachael

"Could I get a Killian's please?" a low, slightly rough voice asked.

Rachael Bradford turned, surprised by the way the sound made her skin prickle and heat.

"Sure thing," she responded automatically, reaching for a cold bottle. She removed the cap and slid it across the bar to him. She looked up and blinked in surprise at the man to whom the voice belonged. He was tall—she had to look up at him to meet his eyes—and his hands were braced on the edge of the bar. His hair fell forward into his eyes, and it was longish and messy, finger tousled, and dark brown. His eyes were what struck her first, though—a clear shade of blue in the low light. There was a darker ring around them, and Rachael realized she'd been staring too long when he smiled crookedly and spoke.

"Thanks. You mind if I start a tab?"

"Nope, not at all."

Their fingers brushed as he handed Rachael the credit card, and she glanced down automatically at the spot where their fingers had touched. Her skin tingled, and she swallowed hard, vaguely perplexed by her reaction to him.

"It's Reeve Jenkins."

"I'm sorry?" Rachael looked back up at him, and he stepped back, shrugged out of the worn-looking black leather jacket and a blue flannel, and placed them both on the seat beside him. It left him in a bright white T-shirt and an old pair of jeans that looked like they were molded to his body in all the right places. Goddamn, he had a body.

"My name; you looked like you were having trouble reading the name on the card. I need to replace it; it's getting kind of worn."

"Oh, yes." Rachael turned away, grateful that he hadn't realized how much his touch affected her. She swiped the card and handed it back to him. She absently wiped at the bar as she struggled to find something to say. God, and she called herself a bartender. She normally had no trouble making small talk with anyone. A handsome face and great body didn't usually render her mute. She felt a wash of gratitude when a middle-aged man took a seat near the other end of the bar.

"Let me know if you need anything," she threw over her shoulder at Reeve before she walked away.

"Your name, unless you want me to call you sweet cheeks," he called after her.

"It's Rachael," she replied, refusing to look over her shoulder but unable to help the smile that crossed her face.

More people filtered into the bar, and although Rachael couldn't say she forgot about Reeve, she was too busy to focus on him. When she finally turned to ask if he needed another beer, he stood to greet a blond man.

"Grant, hey, I was starting to worry," Reeve said.

"Sorry, shitty day at work."

The guy sighed and reached for Reeve, who moved into his arms. Rachael crossed her fingers that they were siblings, or even just close friends, but when their lips brushed together in a lingering, familiar greeting, she sighed in frustration. Not family and definitely not just friends. *Ahh, well, you win some, you lose some, I guess*, she thought. She tried to convince herself that she wasn't disappointed that Reeve was taken, but it was a lie. He had definitely captured her attention. And his friend—named Grant, apparently—had too.

Grant took a seat next to Reeve, and Rachael moved closer to them, brushing away her disappointment.

"Can I get you anything else, Reeve? Or for you, sir?"

Rachael met Grant's eyes and was intrigued to see they were a light green or brown, maybe some combination of the two. Unusual either way. They were a striking contrast with his dark blond hair and perfect stubbled jaw.

"Sure, gorgeous," he drawled. "I'd do just about anything for a Heineken right now."

Jesus, what was it about these two? Rachael wondered. Grant's slow, honey-drenched drawl had her ready to slide across the bar to taste him. And it looked like neither of them were available, damn it.

"I'll take another, too."

Her breath hitched at the way Reeve's eyes crinkled at the corners when he smiled.

She slid both bottles over to them and felt her heart skip in her chest at the sight of them both grinning. *Do they do this a lot?* she wondered. It really wasn't fair to women everywhere. All of the good-looking ones were taken. She knew that better than anyone here in this bar. Jonah had been married, and Tom had fallen in love with a man. She had such stellar taste in guys.

Tom she couldn't be angry with; until he met Sean, he had been convinced he'd spend the rest of his life with a woman. But still, it had been a bit of a blow to the ego. After all, they were dating at the time. He was a good guy, though, and had done the stand-up thing and admitted his attraction to Sean and broke it off with her before he acted on it. They'd adopted twins and had a sweet little family now. Rachael couldn't begrudge him that.

And Jonah, well, he was just a jackass. Rachael had been furious when, three months after they'd started dating, she found out he was married. She had been pretty turned off dating since. It had been a year and a half since she'd dated anyone, and three years since she'd taken home anyone from the bar.

She looked at Reeve and Grant and sighed again. Oh, well, at least she'd have plenty of inspiration tonight when she went home to her little house and cozied up to her porn collection and vibrator.

Lord, she was pathetic. Twenty-seven years old, a successful business owner, and she still couldn't meet a guy. It wasn't her looks—she knew plenty of guys found her dark hair and blue eyes attractive. She was healthy and fit, and most of the time, she was pretty content when she looked at herself in a mirror. She'd accomplished a lot in less than a decade and was proud of herself for that.

Of course, she was at the bar most nights, squirreled away in her messy office, going through the mountains of paperwork that always seemed to accumulate.

No wonder she had no social life.

Rachael snuck surreptitious glances at the gorgeous men sitting next to each other while she helped other customers. Reeve and Grant looked comfortable together. She saw Reeve lean in and speak in Grant's ear, not angling their heads so their bodies didn't touch but pressing right up against each other. Whatever Reeve said made Grant laugh, and both of their gazes flicked over in her direction.

Ugh, she was just going to drive herself nuts if she kept ogling them, so she turned away, slicing up half a dozen limes and dropping them in the caddy before refilling the maraschino cherries. When she'd finished that, she stood on her tiptoes to re-arrange the bottles displayed behind the bar and re-stock the empties. She tugged the shirt with the name of the bar emblazoned on it down from where it had been creeping up her lower back and pulled up her black skinny jeans for good measure before turning around.

Unable to resist another peek, she glanced over to check on Reeve and Grant. They were still sitting close together, biceps and forearms touching. Grant had removed his brown leather jacket and was wearing a black V-neck T-shirt that made her want to lick the smooth skin of his chest. Reeve lazily spun his empty bottle, and Grant flipped the cap as they talked quietly, their gazes trained on her.

"Shit, sorry, you two want another?" she asked, wondering how long they'd been waiting to get her attention.

"Yeah, but this better be our last, gorgeous, if we're going to be any good to anybody tonight." Grant's drawl was even more pronounced, and Rachael's nipples tightened to a painful hardness.

"You could have gotten my attention," she admonished him. "I was just keeping things stocked."

"That's all right; we were enjoying the show." Reeve grinned at her, a slow smirk that made her body flush and her skin tingle.

She grinned back before the confusion set it. Wait, they were both enjoying it? And why would they enjoy it unless they were both attracted to her? She couldn't quite put all the pieces together with these two. Reeve must have seen her puzzled expression because he smiled even more broadly and winked at her. Grant's easy grin was just as enigmatic, and she shook her head, trying to clear the lust-filled haze that had settled there.

After Rachael brought them their beers, Reeve gently caught her hand in his. "Any chance we could get water too?" His hand was warm, and her skin felt hyper-aware of every millimeter of where he was touching her.

"Of course. Lemon or lime?"

"Any chance I could get both?" Grant drawled.

"Me too," Reeve said, licking his lips.

"Sure thing." Rachael set the waters in front of them and watched two sets of hands wrap around the cold glasses. Reeve's fingers were long and narrow, much like his body. *Although*, she thought as she ogled the way his bicep appeared when he flexed, *he was in damned good shape.* Grant's fingers weren't quite as long, or quite as thin, but they were equally appealing. She couldn't help but wonder if the old adage was true that you could tell the size of a man's cock by the length of his fingers. She'd never had the wherewithal to make a study of it. Not that she'd slept with *that* many men, but there had been a nice handful.

Certainly, never two at once, though.

Rachael could suddenly picture two sets of heated hands trailing across her naked flesh and two hard cocks brushing against her thighs. Her fingers tightened on the bunch of paper napkins she held, and her breath caught in her throat.

"You okay there?" Grant asked softly. She looked down at the crushed napkins and swallowed hard.

"I'm fine." Her voice sounded breathier than usual, but it was steady at least. She tossed the napkins in the trash; they were crumpled beyond repair.

Business picked up all of a sudden, and Rachael found herself too busy to talk to them anymore. She kept an eye on the duo, though, refilling their waters and trying to be subtle as she watched them interact. It was an easy, relaxed relationship, that much was certain. If she hadn't been so disappointed that they were clearly a couple, she would have found it fascinating to watch them interact. She was staring at them when she heard a voice to her left.

"Hey, bitch. You have a line-up."

Rachael turned and smiled at the gorgeous blonde towering over her. "Hey, Jenna."

"Thanks for filling in for me tonight, Rach. I am so ready to be done with classes." Jenna had called Rachael earlier in the week to ask if she could cover some of her shift tonight so she could catch up on homework. She was just a month away from graduation and eager to have it finished. "How's it been?"

"It's fine. It's been steady, but not too crazy. The rush is over." Rachael glanced up at the clock. "It should be quiet 'til last call."

"K." Jenna gently caught Rachael by the elbow, turning their bodies so they were facing away from the bar. "By the way, who the hell are the two ridiculously hot guys?" She discreetly tilted her head to the side.

Rachael laughed, unsurprised that Jenna had noticed them immediately. "Their names are Reeve and Grant, apparently. Very cozy with each other, so I'm guessing they're involved, but they're flirty with me too. I seriously don't know what to make of it."

"Hmm, let me keep an eye out. Or do you want to stay out here?"

"Don't tempt me. I wish I could. Unfortunately, eying them is the most action I'll get all year, but I have a pile of paperwork to tackle." Rachael sighed with annoyance, and Jenna nodded sympathetically. She was disgustingly happy in her relationship with a mechanic named Karl, but she'd commiserated with Rachael about her lack of action in the past year and a half often enough.

"I'll let you know what I see."

"Thanks, Jenna." Rachael grinned at her. She waved as she passed Reeve and Grant to head to her office. They both frowned, almost in unison, and she couldn't help the smile that lit up her face. They were just so damned

49

adorable. Although, the word adorable conjured up images of roly-poly puppies and fuzzy kittens, and there was something so unbearably sexy about them that the two images clashed. But it was sweet how in tune with each other they were.

Rachael sighed and took a seat at her desk, forcing Reeve and Grant from her mind. They made for a fun fantasy but had no place in real life. She had hours of work to do and not enough time to get it done. Hawk Point Tavern didn't run itself.

She tackled the paychecks first. Her employees would want checks to cash soon, and it couldn't wait. Thankfully, she had few employees, and it didn't take overly long to tally hours and make out the checks. She had moved on to sorting order invoices for the month when she heard a soft knock on her partially open door. Thinking it was Jenna or Tyler—the other bartender on tonight—she absentmindedly called out, "Come in."

"Excuse me," a low, sexy voice replied.

Rachael's head shot up, and she was startled to see Reeve peering in the door.

"I, uh, hey. Um, hi, Reeve," she stuttered. She cleared her throat. "Come in."

He stepped into the room and pushed the door nearly closed. "Can I talk to you for a sec?"

"Uh, sure." She frowned, puzzled by what he might want but not entirely displeased to have him in her office either. She stood and walked around the desk, leaning back against it and looking up to meet his gaze. "Is there a problem with your bill? Or something else I can help you with?"

He gave her a slow, sexy smirk. "I certainly hope so."

Rachael stared at him, waiting for him to continue, but he was silent. His gaze raked over her body, and she felt heat building between her legs at the slow, frank perusal of her body. By the glittering, heated gaze of his eyes, Rachael could see he liked what he saw. Her jeans and T-shirt were hardly high fashion, but Reeve didn't appear to have any complaints. Besides, Rachael knew she had a tight body, and the jeans showed off her ass nicely.

"What can I help you with?" she asked, her voice breathless.

"Well, you see, I came here looking to have a drink with a good friend, nothing more, but I found something else I'm interested in."

"I'm … I'm sorry?"

Reeve stepped closer until he was just a foot from her, and she felt her heart speed up in her chest.

"What's that?" Rachael repeated when he didn't reply immediately.

"You." The word was simple, but it did nothing to clear up her confusion.

"But … but what about Grant?" she asked. "I mean, it looked like you two were together, and I—I don't want to cause any problems or get in the way of anything."

Reeve moved so he was standing in front of her, booted feet on either side of her crossed ones. He leaned in, breathing softly against her cheek, and she wet her lips reflexively.

"It's pretty simple actually," Reeve purred in her ear. "Grant and I hook up occasionally, and we are both very attracted to you." His lips brushed the sensitive outer shell, and she shivered.

Bi then. Her experiences with Tom made her a little leery of bi guys, but it's not like she was going to get involved with them beyond a quick—or maybe not so quick—roll in the sheets, she thought. This was a one-off. It wasn't like she was going to see them after tonight, so she might as well enjoy it while she had the opportunity.

"You aren't in a relationship with him?" she said aloud. The last thing she wanted was to get involved with another cheater. Jonah had been more than enough, *thankyouverymuch*.

Reeve shrugged. "We've been friends for a long time, but it's nothing exclusive. We keep things fluid."

"So how would this work?" Rachael asked, her voice going a little breathless as she imagined what could play out if she said yes. "We'd have a threesome?"

51

"That is entirely up to you. If you're only attracted to one of us, the other will step aside; although, we'd both be very disappointed. And somehow, I don't think that's the case, is it?"

"No, I'm definitely attracted to both of you," Rachael admitted. Reeve wrapped an arm around her lower back and pulled her flush against his body.

"Then how we fuck"—he skimmed a hand down her back to cup the lower curve of her ass—"is up for negotiation. Whatever you're comfortable with."

She gulped at the images swirling through her brain.

Reeve's lips traced across her cheek. "Ever fucked two guys at once?"

"No," she whispered, her voice shaky.

"I can tell you this; if Grant could slide right into your ass while I fucked your pussy, I think we could make you come harder than you ever have before."

Oh, God. Double penetration. She couldn't deny she'd been fantasizing about that for a damn long time. Her browser history could certainly attest to that. But making the fantasy a reality? That had never really crossed her mind.

She let out a shaky moan, and Reeve continued. "But if that isn't something you're comfortable with, there are a thousand ways it can be pleasurable for all of us. As long as you don't mind Grant and I enjoying each other in front of you."

"No," she answered hoarsely. "I think that would be incredible to watch. And the idea of you both inside me? I can't tell you how turned on that makes me."

Reeve moved his hand to the front of her shirt and brushed a thumb across her very hard nipple. "You don't have to tell me, sweet cheeks; I can feel it."

Rachael moaned and clamped her hands on Reeve's biceps, gripping them to stay upright.

"Starting without me, are you, Reeve?" Grant drawled from the doorway, and Rachael jerked in surprise. She had been so focused on the feel of Reeve touching her that she hadn't been paying any attention to her surroundings. "He's always so impatient."

Reeve nuzzled her hairline with his lips as she stared at Grant. "You wouldn't have been able to resist either, Grant."

"True enough." Grant's gaze was heated as he stared at them. "I'm guessin' she didn't turn you down."

"No, I didn't," Rachael admitted. Her body thrummed with excitement as she said the words that simultaneously thrilled and terrified her. "I want it all."

Grant's eyes flared with a hot and hungry look then settled to a low smolder that made her ache. She crooked a finger at him, and he crossed the room to them.

"Then I suppose I should allow myself a little taste." Grant put one hand on Reeve's back and another one on hers. They stood on either of side of her, and she found herself surrounded by tall, warm, distinctly aroused male bodies that made her heart pound in her chest and her knees go weak.

Reeve gently tilted her head so she was staring at Grant, who leaned down slowly to press their lips together. It was a soft, warm, slow kiss. Easy and without demand. She welcomed it. He pulled back after a moment and stared down at her, a crooked smile on his face.

"Have you tasted Rachael yet, Reeve?" Grant asked, stroking her back.

"No." Reeve's voice was low and heavy with desire.

"She's delicious."

Grant cupped the back of her head in his hand and guided her until her lips met Reeve's. His kiss was rougher, deeper, and it set her skin ablaze with desire.

"Unless we're going to continue this right here, I think we'd best stop," Grant said. But his lips continued to move down her neck, and Reeve's joined his on the other side. Rachael groaned then nearly jumped a foot when she heard Jenna's voice in the doorway. "I am so jealous of you right now, Rach."

What the hell is up with people startling me today? she wondered as she whipped around to face Jenna and nearly fell when she got caught in the tangle of limbs around her. Reeve and Grant both steadied her.

"Shit, sorry, Jenna," Rachael said, trying to regain her composure. She wasn't used to her employees catching her fooling around with a guy. Much less two.

"You'd better not be. I do have a quick question for you, though, before I leave you in those four very capable-looking hands."

Reeve and Grant immediately stepped back, and Rachael walked over to Jenna.

"Please, please tell me you're going home with them both," Jenna said quietly, too low for them to hear.

Rachael laughed softly. "Yes," she admitted. "It looks like I am." A jolt of adrenaline shot through her at the thought.

She had never been uptight about sex, but *this* was something entirely new for her. It was thrilling and just a little bit terrifying. It was reckless and maybe a little bit dangerous, but she wanted Reeve and Grant. And every instinct she had told her she could trust them. Despite her recent abysmal relationship history, she was actually quite good at reading people. She glanced over at them to see Grant whispering in Reeve's ear as Reeve caressed Grant's arm.

"I love Karl, but fuck me, I'm jealous," Jenna said under her breath. "God, you are a lucky bitch. If you don't call me in the morning with the details, I will beat you to within an inch of your life."

"I'll call; I'll call," Rachael reassured her, laughing. "Now, what did you need to ask? Or was that your question?"

"No, I just wanted to know if you'd be in tomorrow or if you wanted me to grab the early shift for you. I can; I don't have any plans, and I totally owe you one for tonight."

"You don't have to," Rachael protested, but as she glanced behind her, she caught a glimpse of the two beautiful men waiting for her, undressing her with their eyes.

Jenna laughed. "You won't be able to walk tomorrow, woman. Let me work it for you."

"All right," Rachael agreed, glad that she'd offered.

Jenna hugged her and left with another muttered "lucky bitch." Rachael turned to face Reeve and Grant. "Well, it looks like I'm done here for the night. I'm ready to leave, if you are."

"Absolutely," Grant responded.

"Where are we going?" Reeve asked. "Grant lives on the other side of town, but I have an apartment nearby. Or would you rather go to your place?"

Rachael shrugged. "Your apartment is fine, Reeve."

"All right."

She swiped her beat-up leather coat from the back of her desk chair, snagged her purse, and gestured the men through the door of her office. She locked it behind her, and they followed her out the rear of the building to where she was parked.

It was a frosty November night and figuring out the logistics of getting to Reeve's apartment took a little while. Rachael shivered in the cold air as they decided to leave Grant's truck at the bar and that she would follow Reeve to his place. Grant rubbed his hands up and down her arms to keep her warm as Reeve gave her the address and basic directions. They each gave her a searing kiss before she unlocked her car door. She'd just turned the key in the ignition when Grant slid into the passenger seat. Rachael turned to look at him.

He gave her a disarming grin and spoke. "It occurred to me that it might be easier if I just rode with you, then you won't have to worry about following Reeve. The man drives like a bat out of hell."

"Oh, sure," she said with a soft laugh.

"If you're all right with it, that is. I don't want to intrude or make you uncomfortable."

"It was a good idea." Rachael smiled at him and put her car in gear. He buckled his seatbelt and sat back, his hands loosely resting on his thighs.

She wet her lips as nerves erupted in her stomach. She was excited about what was going to happen, but alone in the car with Grant, she had no idea how to behave.

Rachael pulled out onto the street behind Reeve and tapped her fingertips on the steering wheel, unsure what to say. She jabbed at the power button to turn on the radio, relaxing a fraction when the sounds of classic rock filled her car. At least, it wasn't silent anymore. She snuck a glance out of the corner of her eye at Grant and saw him staring straight ahead. He didn't look nervous or uncomfortable; in fact, from the way he was sitting, he looked quite relaxed. She looked back at the road then found her gaze wandering to him again. This time, their gazes met, and she quickly looked away.

Grant gently touched her upper thigh, skimming across the denim. "Hey, you okay?"

She nodded and swallowed hard. "Just a little bit nervous, I guess."

"What exactly are you nervous about?" he asked softly.

"It's just kind of … new to me, I guess. I've never done this."

"Gone home with a guy from the bar?"

"That I've done," she admitted. "But I've certainly never gone home with two guys from the bar in the same night."

"I have." Grant grinned at her, and she laughed, relaxing a little at his comment.

"With Reeve?" she asked.

"Yes. A few times. With both men and women. It's not a regular thing for us, but it has happened before."

"How did it go?"

He shrugged. "One time, a girl decided she wasn't really as okay as she thought she was with it, so she kinda bolted out of bed in the middle of our fun and left. That was … odd. But Reeve and I managed to salvage the evening. On the other hand, we had a few other encounters that went quite well. It was a pleasurable experience for all. I think we can do right by you."

"So, you two know what you're doing?" she pressed.

He grinned at me. "I like to think so, yes."

"Is there a money-back guarantee?" she asked teasingly, finally starting to relax.

"Hot damn," Grant said. "You mean you're going to pay us for this? Hell, we were just gonna do it for free."

Rachael laughed, his humor relaxing her further. Grant chuckled too, and he put his hand on her upper thigh, keeping it there this time. "I swear to you, Rachael, if you say stop, we stop. No matter what. I know it's a scary situation to put yourself in, but you can trust us. We will never do anything you aren't one hundred percent okay with."

"I appreciate it," she said. "You seem like good guys, but the situation is kind of nerve-racking."

"I completely understand." He squeezed her thigh gently. "I swear you have nothing to worry about. We only want you to do something if you're comfortable with it. We won't be offended if you change your mind either. Tonight is about bringing each other pleasure." He rubbed his thumb along Rachael's inseam, and she swallowed hard. With her nerves fading, desire was growing again. She glanced over at him when they stopped at a light, and he smiled at her. "I promise, nothing but pleasure."

Rachael nodded, and when the light turned green, he pointed to the street to the right. She could see Reeve's taillights a few car lengths ahead. She followed them a short way down the road and into the entrance of an apartment complex. Grant directed her to the visitor parking area as Reeve slid into a numbered spot. She grabbed her purse, and Grant escorted her over to where Reeve stood, his hand pressed gently to her lower back. Reeve smiled at the two of them, and they followed him up to his apartment.

It was a large sprawling complex, and his place was located on the second floor, accessible from an indoor stairwell. Grant slid a hand under her leather jacket and slowly rubbed his thumb against her lower back over the thin fabric of her shirt while Reeve unlocked the door.

Rachael took note of the apartment number and grabbed her phone as she followed Reeve inside. Grant threw himself down on the couch, and she sat next to him a little more gingerly.

"Uh, I'm going to text the address to Jenna; I hope you understand …" Rachael said.

Reeve nodded and gently tossed his things on the coffee table. "Of course. Do whatever you need to feel safe and comfortable. We have nothing to hide."

Rachael nodded and sent Jenna the message. It was returned almost immediately.

You better call me tomorrow with the deets, bitch. XOXO

Rachael smiled and tucked her phone in her purse, really looking around Reeve's apartment for the first time. His place wasn't overly large, but it was fairly neat and nicely decorated. It looked like a man with a good eye had carefully amassed a collection of well-loved items. There was a buttery brown leather sofa and a couple comfortable-looking chairs grouped around a low wood coffee table. It held a couple large-format books, some coasters, and the items from his pocket. There were a few photographs on the walls and a TV on the wall across from the couch.

Reeve used a remote to turn on the stereo system. Something bluesy and mellow began to play.

Once Rachael had finished looking around, she fiddled with the silver ring she wore on her right hand, wanting to say something but not really sure how to proceed from here. What was the protocol for starting a threesome? Still grieving her parents' deaths, she'd missed out on a lot of the opportunities her friends in college had taken advantage of.

"Would you like a drink?" Grant asked.

She nodded gratefully. "That would be nice."

She grabbed one of the coffee table books and perused it while Reeve and Grant disappeared into the other room. It was a book on local architecture, and although she'd picked it up to try to keep her nerves at bay, she soon found herself immersed. It was really quite fascinating.

"Tequila okay?" Reeve called out.

"Is it any good?" she asked, turning toward his voice.

"Don Julio 1942," he answered, peering around the corner at her with a cheeky grin.

She grinned broadly in response. "Oh, *hell* yes."

It was a pricey bottle of liquor, and although she stocked it at the bar, it had been a long time since she'd drank it herself. In a few minutes, Reeve and Grant came out carrying the bottle, three shot glasses, some sliced limes, and a small bowl of salt. They took seats on either side of her, and Grant expertly poured the shots.

"Nicely done," she teased, and his answering chuckle sent a warm flush through her.

She took a moment to soak in the feeling of them beside her. Their warm thighs pressed against her own, and the scent of their respective colognes mingled in the air, making her feel dizzy with lust. She licked her lips, wanting to taste both of them again, her mind whirling with the possibilities of what the night would bring. Grant set a shot down in front of her, and she smiled gratefully at him.

Although, she was eager to see where the evening would lead, she was slightly apprehensive as well, and she knew tequila shots would loosen them all up. They methodically lined the drinks up and prepared the salt and limes. After the shots had been consumed and the limes had been bitten, Grant leaned back against the arm of the sofa and smiled at her.

"I have a suggestion."

"What's that?" she asked.

"How do you feel about body shots?"

Rachael smiled. It was a bit juvenile, but under the circumstances, she couldn't think of a better suggestion. It would be a fantastic icebreaker and just the thing to get the evening rolling. "Sure," she agreed.

"What do you think, Reeve?" Grant asked.

"I'm in."

"Who goes first?" she asked.

Grant shrugged. "I'm game. Coffee table?"

Reeve nodded, and Rachael helped him clear it off, placing the items on the end table. Grant stood and pulled off his shirt without any hesitation.

Grant's stomach was flat, and there was a narrow line of light brown hair trailing down into the waistband of his pants as he undid them and pushed them a bit lower. A light smattering of golden, curly hairs dusted his pecs, and Rachael licked her lips. Reeve gave her a knowing grin and winked. She shrugged in response.

Grant carefully lay back across the table, and Rachael knelt on the floor between the couch and table while Reeve followed suit on the other side.

Rachael dragged the lime along the bony ridge of Grant's hip and sprinkled salt lightly across it. Her head swam at the scent of the leather from his belt and warm male skin. She took her time and lapped at the smooth skin there, teasing him a little with her tongue. Grant's body tensed and his breathing sped up. She glanced at Reeve to see him watching her intently, a lime between his teeth. Grant's stomach clenched under her fingers, and he sighed when she sat back and tossed down the tequila shot Reeve handed her. She leaned across Grant to suck the lime juice from Reeve's mouth. After a moment, he pulled away long enough to pluck the lime wedge from his mouth and toss it aside before capturing her lips in a searing kiss. They pulled back, panting, and were met with a heated gaze from Grant that made her stomach flutter.

God, this is going to be so good, she thought.

Reeve took Grant's place, and when Grant knelt beside him, Rachael felt the heat spread through her body at the image of two beautiful men touching each other. By the time Grant slammed his shot and sucked the lime from Rachael's mouth, she was panting and eager for them both. When they helped her lay down on the table and each took a spot on either side of her, she couldn't slow her eager breathing. With a gentle motion, they slid her shirt up and off. The lime juice was shockingly cold on her breasts, and she let out a quiet gasp. Two warm, wet mouths bent to capture her nipples, and she arched up off the table in response.

Two hands ran from her knee, up her denim-clad thighs, and met at the juncture. She gasped and ground against them, not entirely coherent anymore. With their free hands, they slammed their shots and looked down at her with identical expression of desire.

"Please," Rachael gasped. "Please, I need you. *Now*."

Reeve stood first and took her hand, leading her toward the back of the apartment. Grant followed quickly behind. Once inside the bedroom, Reeve turned on a low lamp beside the bed. Rachael didn't have time to look at the room before he reached for her.

He immediately stripped her jeans and panties from her. She eagerly reached for the button on Reeve's jeans and heard the jingle of Grant's belt behind her. Once they were all naked, Rachael found herself surrounded by warm flesh from both sides and sighed at the feeling of four large, slightly rough hands caressing her. It was an almost overwhelming feeling at first, and she let her head fall back against Grant's shoulder. With her eyes closed, she gave in to the dizzying feel of hands and lips and tongues and teeth across her body.

At some point, they gently led her over to the bed, and her head swam at the mixture of tequila and the feel of both of them touching her.

Grant positioned himself between Rachael's thighs while Reeve played with her nipples. And then they switched. They were different, but both so, so good. Grant's touch was a little rougher, making her cry out, but Reeve's softer, teasing licks across her pussy made her shudder.

Rachael's awareness shrank to the two men on the bed and the way they made her feel. She closed her eyes, greedily soaking in every soft lick of the tongue and every gentle pinch of her nipple.

They flipped her onto her hands and knees so she straddled Reeve, facing his feet, and Grant positioned himself behind her. She tried to suck Reeve's cock, but the dual stimulation from both of their mouths proved overwhelming. When Grant began a thorough assault on her asshole with his tongue, and Reeve carefully grazed his teeth across her clit, she came, long and loud. She shuddered and cried out, again and again, until her thighs were weak and trembling. She came until her clit became super-sensitive, and she had to push Reeve's head away.

"Please," she begged finally.

"Please what?" Reeve asked. He smirked at her from between her thighs.

"I just need a minute," Rachael gasped.

They shifted, gently laying her against the pillows at the head of the bed, and her dazed eyes finally focused on the two of them staring at her with concerned expressions. Rachael shook her head to clear it and smiled reassuringly at them.

"I feel amazing; I just need a minute, okay?" She waved in their general direction. "Feel free to play among yourselves while I watch."

Grant slid up onto the bed from where he'd been kneeling on the floor. On their knees, he and Reeve reached for each other, the long, hard lines of their bodies meshing perfectly together. She watched them kiss, their tongues tangling, sharing the taste of her arousal between them. Despite the aching pleasure they had already given her, she found herself shifting on the bed as she watched as Grant licked Reeve's flat, small nipples and Reeve's fingers dug into Grant's firmly muscled ass. Their hard cocks rubbed together, and she bit her lip at the sight. She'd watched gay porn a few times but never expected to see it playing out live in front of her.

Reeve pushed Grant onto the bed beside her and lowered his head to Grant's cock. Reeve swallowed it down but not before Rachael noticed that she had been right about the difference in size between them, although neither was anything to sneer at. They were both circumcised and beautifully made, smooth and long and just thick enough.

Without conscious thought, she rubbed her pussy. It was slick with arousal. From her previous orgasms or the show in front of her, she wasn't sure, but it didn't really matter. She gently dragged some of the moisture up to her clitoris, careful of how sensitive it was.

Reeve cupped Grant's balls and gently tugged on them while he devoured his cock. Grant let out the sexiest moan she had ever heard. They were right beside her. She could feel the heat from Grant's skin against hers, and Reeve's arm brushed her thigh as he worked to bring Grant pleasure. Grant's hands tangled in Reeve's hair, tugging roughly. Reeve let out a low, guttural groan around Grant's cock, which made her frig her clit a little faster.

Reeve pulled back for a moment before plunging down again. Rachael sighed at the view of the glistening length of Grant's cock disappearing into Reeve's mouth again. Grant turned to look at her, his gaze heated as he fumbled to take her hand. She looked back at Reeve as he roughly sucked Grant, feeling a thrum of connection to both of them despite the fact that Grant was touching her in a completely platonic way at the moment.

"Fuck, his mouth ... Rachael, he's so good at sucking cock," Grant gasped.

"It's incredible to watch," Rachael admitted, her voice coming out huskier than usual.

"Is it turnin' you on?" Grant asked.

"You have no idea." Rachael lifted their joined hands and guided his fingers between her legs.

"Mmm, you're all slick and swollen." Two of his fingers slid into her. "Feels so good. I can't wait to feel it on my cock."

Rachael moaned and arched her hips to meet his touch, hampered by the awkward angle where they were joined. "Grant," she whimpered, not even sure what she was asking for.

"Oh, gorgeous, you are so ready for us. Do you want to get fucked now?"

"Yes," she gasped.

Reeve slowly slid off Grant's cock and grinned at her. "I think you better take over, Rachael. He's so close to coming. I don't think he'll last much longer, but I bet he'd love to come in your mouth."

Rachael nodded vigorously, eager to bring them pleasure like they'd given her. Reeve pulled a box of condoms from the bedside table, along with a bottle of lube. Reeve sheathed his cock in a condom, and they gently slid her to the middle of the bed while they took a spot on either side of her.

They both reached for her, hands caressing and bringing her pleasure, every inch of her body an erogenous zone under their talented touches. Reeve tilted her head to the side, and he kissed her deeply, his tongue wet and warm and tasting faintly of her arousal. She caressed Grant's cock. Although the angle was awkward, he moaned softly at the gentle strokes of her hand. She felt two sets of fingers exploring between her thighs, and she parted them, eager for their touch.

She quickly lost track of who was doing what, and it wasn't until Reeve settled himself between her thighs and Grant gently rubbed the head of his cock across her lips that she snapped back to herself. Grant was off to one side, kneeling by her head, bracing his arm against the headboard.

Rachael lapped at the sticky pre-come at the tip. She couldn't see his face, but he responded with a groan that encouraged her to take him into her mouth. She did, eagerly in fact, and Grant began to gently rock forward. He had all the control, but he didn't push her. Rachael reached up and wrapped her hand around his ass, pulling him deeper into her mouth.

"You ready?" Reeve asked, and she let go of Grant to reach down and grip Reeve's arm and let him know she was. When he pushed forward slowly, she gasped, which made Grant's cock slide deeper, nearly gagging her. After he pulled back, she quickly regained her momentum.

Soon, Grant came in her mouth with a couple of hard spurts that she greedily swallowed down. She licked him clean until he groaned and pulled away, falling back onto the bed, his eyes glued on Reeve fucking her. "Christ, the sight of your dick disappearing into her pussy ... fuck, that's hot, Reeve."

"She feels so good," Reeve moaned. "I'm not gonna last much longer."

Rachael focused on Reeve then, feeling him working inside of her. He glanced up at her, and his blue eyes glittered darkly. He lifted her thighs and hooked her legs over his shoulders, driving into her with a deep thrust that made her see stars. He set up a quick, hard rhythm, and she felt her core tighten as an orgasm built inside her

"I'm coming," she called out, scrabbling for a grip on the sheets bunched beneath her. Reeve gritted his teeth and clenched his jaw as she spasmed around him. She gasped and cried out, her back arching as they both came. Reeve ground against her as he rode out his own orgasm. He lowered her thighs to the bed and collapsed on top of her, bracing his weight on his elbows.

"Fuck, Rachael," he sighed against her mouth. She kissed him as they slowly came down from their orgasms. He carefully pulled out of her, and they both turned to Grant. He grinned at them, his hand wrapped around his cock, which had begun to stir to life again.

"Damn, you two are hot to watch."

"So are you," she said, weakly pulling herself closer to him as Reeve discarded the condom. Grant cradled the back of her head in his hand, and they kissed deeply.

After a moment, he pulled back to say, "I'm gonna fuck you next, gorgeous. I hope you're ready."

Exhausted but still incredibly turned on, all Rachael could do was nod. Go big or go home, right? When was she ever going to have the chance to get her brains fucked out like this again?

Grant took Reeve's place, his eyes locked on hers as he rolled on a condom and thrust inside of her. She gasped and arched up to meet him. Reeve leaned down to give her a quick kiss before he stood. He scooped up the bottle of lube and a condom, then walked to the foot of the bed. He stood behind Grant, running his hands across Grant's back then down to cup his ass. Grant groaned loudly as Reeve knelt.

Rachael strained to see, but Grant blocked her view. He grinned at her. "Wanna know what he's doing?"

She nodded eagerly, and Grant began to narrate while he moved inside her, beginning a slow, steady rhythm.

"Ooooh, God, Rachael, he's holding me open with his thumbs so he can tease me with his tongue. It feels so damned good," Grant panted.

"One of his hands is playing with my balls now, gently tugging. He knows that drives me crazy." Grant continued the deep even strokes, but his breathing picked up and began to grow ragged. Grant closed his eyes and breathed deeply as Reeve continued.

"So good. Goddamn it, he's good at that. Rimming me. Your tight little pussy around my cock and Reeve's tongue on my ass. *Fuck*."

She felt Reeve's fingertips brush her lips as his fingers caressed Grant, and she cried out. "Harder, Grant, please," she begged.

Grant began to move faster and harder within her, and she gasped and gripped the sheets beside her, her skin developing a light sheen of sweat as they fucked. Grant stilled and threw his head back in pleasure, a low, desperate moan leaving him.

"Christ, he has a finger inside of me. Fuck, please, Reeve, just fuck me. I want you inside of me when I come in Rachael," he panted.

Rachael shuddered at the image his words created. Grant groaned and stilled her with a hand on her leg. She forced herself to lay quietly under him as Reeve stood and leaned over Grant's back. He winked at her, and Grant moaned.

"Two fingers in him now. He's almost ready for my cock," Reeve said, and he tugged Grant's head to the side, one hand gripping his hair. "I can smell both of you, and it's making me so fucking hot. I need to feel you. Rachael, are you close? Grant and I aren't going to last long once I get inside him."

She nodded, whimpering a little as Grant shifted inside her, his gritted jaw the only indication he was as close to coming as she was. "Yes," she gasped.

Reeve bit and licked along Grant's neck, and she ran a hand up Grant's arm, trying to soothe him.

Grant grunted and his eyes closed tightly, his arms shaking a little from the strain.

"I'm ready. I need you now, Reeve," he said between gritted teeth. "Rachael, it's going to be hard and rough, and I don't think I can last long."

"Fine by me," she managed.

Reeve stepped away for a moment, and Grant let out a relieved sigh. He leaned down and kissed her, the movement stimulating her clit. She was dimly aware of Reeve rolling a condom on and slicking lube on his cock. And she gasped out loud when Reeve pushed into Grant. The sound of them both groaning filled the room, and she involuntarily clenched down around Grant.

"Goddamn it," he cried. "You both feel so fucking good."

Reeve moved slowly at first, and each deliberate thrust into Grant pushed Grant further into her. Soon there were just the sounds of slippery skin slapping together, their cries and groans, and the slick sound of fucking.

She felt the orgasm roll through her, and she clenched around Grant, her fingers digging into his shoulders. Grant held out longer than she expected, but when Reeve picked up the pace and really began to thrust hard, Grant cried out.

Rachael felt him shudder against her, and Reeve followed just a moment later. After pulling carefully out of Grant, Reeve fell onto the bed beside her, and Grant pulled out and followed suit. She curled up with her head on Grant's shoulder, and he turned to face her, his eyes glazed, his chest heaving with exertion. Reeve took care of both of the condoms and brought back two soft cloths to wipe them clean. He disappeared into the bathroom and returned a few moments later to join them on the bed. He stretched out next to Rachael and reached over her body to pull the three of them closer.

"Was that good for you?" Grant asked when they were all curled together.

Rachael let out a breathless, shocked laugh. "That was the best fucking sex I've ever had. Everything tonight is just … so much more than anything I've ever experienced. You have no idea."

Grant chuckled, and Reeve propped himself up on his elbow. "I'm pretty sure Grant does. I've never seen him come that hard."

"Damn, having both of you at once was just so incredible." Grant kissed her softly, his tongue gently stroking hers before he stretched to do the same to Reeve.

"I love watching you two kiss," Rachael admitted, feeling the tingling in her pussy begin again. God, had she ever been this insatiable? But who could blame her with two beautiful men like that? "It's such a turn on."

Grant sat up and held up a hand. "Hold it there, gorgeous. I don't know about Reeve but I need a few minutes to recharge. Think you can give us poor men some time to refuel and recover?"

Rachael pouted. "Well, I suppose if I have to …"

"Thank the Lord," Grant muttered. "You could kill a man. Not that I'd complain if I went that way, but I'm not gonna be much use to you dead. And it's a hell of a lot more fun if we can keep goin' later."

She laughed and glanced over at Reeve. "Is he always like this?"

Reeve grinned. "Always. But I've found that feeding him usually improves his mood. What do you say we throw together a bite to eat so we can refuel for the next round?"

She stretched. "Sounds good to me."

She clambered off the wide bed, but when she reached for her clothes, Reeve stopped her. "Do you have to cover up those lovely tits?"

"These?" She cupped her breasts in her hands and batted her lashes at him, feeling playful.

Reeve and Grant both groaned. "Yeah, those," Grant said in a choked voice.

She giggled, but a shiver skittered over her skin, pebbling it with goosebumps and ending that debate. "Without your body heat to keep me warm, I'm afraid I am a little cold, boys. Think you can compromise and let me wear *something*?"

A white T-shirt appeared in front of her, dangling from Reeve's finger. "If it's my shirt, I think I can agree to that."

"Deal." She slid the shirt over her head, inhaling the scent of Reeve's cologne. *Mmm, that is nice.* The shirt hung off her small frame, ending mid-thigh and slipping down over one shoulder.

She glanced over to see Grant dressed in a pair of gray boxers and Reeve in snug black boxer briefs. Well, at least, she wasn't going to be the only one half-naked.

"Bathroom's through there, right?" she asked, pointing to the door on the far side of the room. It had been a while since she'd last had sex and after this much ... yeah, she wasn't about to risk a UTI.

Reeve nodded. "Feel free to rummage through drawers or the linen closet and borrow anything you need."

"Thanks." She walked toward the bathroom, noticing the ache in her thighs and the soreness in her lower abs for the first time. Damn, she couldn't remember the last time she'd been fucked so thoroughly. *Of course, it helps to have two do it,* she thought with a little smile.

Rachael stepped into the bathroom and flipped on the light. She caught a glimpse of her reflection in the mirror and stopped in her tracks. She looked well-fucked of course, with messy hair and mascara smeared around her eyes. But there was color in her cheeks and sparkle in her eyes that she hadn't seen in a long time. And her smile wouldn't quit.

She looked *happy.*

She'd be the first to admit she had a pretty damn good life, but it had gotten awfully boring. She hadn't realized what a rut she'd been in lately. Running the bar, going home to eat and sleep, the occasional night out with friends … it wasn't bad … but it wasn't exciting either.

Clearly, a threesome was just the thing to add a spark to her life. She stifled a chuckle and turned on the tap to run a little warm water. She left the bathroom a few minutes later, bladder empty, her hair untangled, and the worst of the raccoon eyes washed away.

On the way to the kitchen, Rachael made a detour into the living room to grab her phone. She fired off a quick message to Jenna.

*Best. Decision. Ever. Night's not over, and I feel amazing already. Deets tomorrow, I promise. *mwah**

She hit send and slipped the phone back into her purse without waiting for a reply. She wandered toward the kitchen and found the men good-naturedly arguing. She paused in the doorway and watched them for a moment. The same easy comradery she'd noticed in her bar was still present, but they'd let down any remaining barriers. Grant slid a hand along Reeve's back as he slipped past to open the refrigerator. Reeve squeezed Grant's ass as he bent to retrieve a cutting board from the cabinet.

Grant seemed completely at home in Reeve's kitchen, and they casually danced around each other as they navigated the space like they'd done it a thousand times before. It sent a wistful feeling through her as she wondered what that kind of familiarity would be like. She couldn't remember the last time she'd felt that with anyone, not even her ex-boyfriends.

Grant turned and his face lit up when he spotted her. "Hey there, gorgeous. I was just about to send out a search party."

Rachael pushed away the sudden and unwanted melancholy, determined to enjoy the rest of the evening. "Just enjoying the show," she joked as she walked toward him.

Grant wrapped his arms around her, and she squealed when he lifted her and set her on the counter. "I don't have any underwear on!" she protested as she shifted to make sure Reeve's T-shirt covered her nether regions.

Grant leered at her. "All the better!"

"But the counters!" she protested.

Reeve rolled his eyes. "This kitchen has seen far worse than your pretty little butt. Trust me. It certainly wouldn't be the first time Grant got frisky in here."

Rachael giggled.

"Enough making fun of Grant," Grant said. "Let's talk food. Do you want a full meal or snacks?"

Rachael thought for a moment. She wasn't starving, but a bite of something sounded nice.

"A full meal would probably put me to sleep," she admitted.

"Snacks it is!" Reeve said.

Rachael laughed.

"Crackers and cheese?" Reeve offered. "I have grapes too, I think. Some brownies, if you have a sweet tooth."

"Works for me," Rachael agreed. "Now can I get down off the counter and help?"

"Hell no!" he said with a grin. "You stay right there and look pretty for us."

She shrugged and smiled to herself, crossing her legs as she watched Reeve and Grant move around the kitchen.

"So do threesomes with you guys always involve dinner and a show?" she joked, but a little stab of jealousy went through her again, wondering about the women—and men, she reminded herself—who had been in her place before. And no doubt would be in the future.

Reeve stilled, a large knife in his hand. "No, actually." His tone was thoughtful. "We've had a few people join us, but it's not usually like this."

He and Grant exchanged a look that Rachael couldn't decipher. "What do you mean?" she asked.

Grant stepped closer and ran his hands up her thighs under the shirt she wore. "Let's just say Reeve and I have had some pretty great times in the bedroom with a guest, but we don't feed them midnight snacks or want them to spend the night. We have our fun, they go home, and that's that."

"So, I'm not overstepping my bounds if I stay the night then?" She felt oddly nervous.

"No!" Grant and Reeve answered in almost perfect unison, and Reeve set down his knife and walked over to her and Grant.

"I like having you here in my apartment," Reeve said. "It feels ... comfortable with you here."

Grant nodded. "Not to put down anyone else we were with—that's not my style—but you just fit better."

Rachael swallowed, feeling an odd lump in her throat. Why it should matter so much, she wasn't sure. "I feel comfortable with you two as well," she admitted. "I thought this might be awkward but ..."

"... this feels surprisingly easy, doesn't it?" Reeve said.

Rachael nodded.

He leaned in and gave her a quick but thorough kiss. Grant did the same to her, then turned and kissed Reeve. She sighed as she watched them.

Grant pulled back and wagged a finger at Reeve. "No more distracting me. You have to feed me before you fuck me again."

Reeve snorted. "I'm pretty sure it's Rachael's turn to be in the middle." But he returned to chopping cubes of cheese.

Grant winked at her. "Snacks, then a Rachael sandwich."

She giggled and desperately tried to think of anything but the images Grant's words conjured. If she wasn't careful, she'd leave a wet spot on the counter.

In no time at all, there was a pile of delicious-looking food on a big plate. Grant held out a hand and helped her down.

"That looks delicious," she said, snagging a cube of what appeared to be cheddar off the plate in Reeve's hand.

"No eating until we're in the bedroom." Grant swatted her ass, and she yelped and giggled. She nibbled on the cheese cube as they walked back to the bedroom, surprised by how relaxed and comfortable she felt. Here she was, half-naked with two virtual strangers, who'd fucked the hell out of her already, about to eat a snack in bed before going at it again.

She really had missed out in college by having to be the responsible adult. She thought about most of her fellow college students at the time and how immature they'd been. Then again, maybe it was better that she was getting to explore this side of herself when she was a little older.

"What are you thinkin' about so hard?" Grant asked.

Rachael realized she'd paused in the doorway of the bedroom. Reeve and Grant were both stretched out on the bed with the plate of food between them. Water glasses sat on the nightstand. "Oh." She laughed softly and took a seat on the bed. "I got lost in my thoughts. I was thinking that I missed a lot of opportunities to do this"—she waved her hand—"in college because of my parents, but I think maybe it worked out for the best. I'm mature enough to really enjoy it now."

Reeve nodded thoughtfully before his forehead furrowed with a frown. "What do you mean about your parents?"

"Oh." She glanced down. "Uh, my parents died in a car accident when I was nineteen. I took a while off to deal with that and get all their affairs in order. After that, I finished business classes and opened the bar with the insurance money."

Reeve set his hand on her bare leg, his fingers long and elegant-looking. "I'm sorry to hear that. I'm sure they would be very proud of what you've accomplished."

Grant's blunter, stronger fingers landed on her knee. "I'm sorry too. I didn't mean to bring up bad memories."

She'd dealt with her parents' deaths a long time ago, but sometimes, the smallest things still caught her by surprise. She blinked back a sheen of tears and forced away the sadness.

"It's okay. You had no way of knowing."

"Do you have any siblings?" Reeve asked, letting go of her to grab some food. She appreciated the reprieve.

Rachael reached for a cracker and set a cube of cheese on it before she shook her head. "Nope. It's just me. My mom had a sister, but they were estranged, so I never met my aunt or her family. And my dad's brother died in the Gulf War."

Grant squeezed her knee. "So it's just you?" He sounded concerned.

"It is. But I have Jenna and Tyler. They're my employees, but they're good friends too. The first few years of running the bar were a struggle, but by the time I turned twenty-four, we were operating in the black, and in the last few years, business has been pretty steady. I have a cozy little house, I can give my employees benefits, and I only have to work behind the bar a couple days a week. I've built a nice little life for myself."

"It sounds like it," Reeve said. He reached out and brushed his thumb against her lower lip.

Rachael cleared her throat. "So, what do you two do? Other than go to bars and pick up women. Well, *people*."

Grant chuckled. "Trust me, that's not a full-time job. Although, if all of them were as incredible as you, I'd be tempted to make it one."

Flustered, Rachael snagged a few grapes. "I hardly think I'm that unusual."

Grant and Reeve exchanged glances. "You might be surprised."

Rachael opened her mouth, but she had no idea how to respond, so she changed the subject. "So what *do* you do?"

"My brother and I own a music store," Reeve said. "We sell pianos, guitars, basses, symphony and marching band instruments … oh, and we offer music lessons."

"I'm an AutoCAD drafter," Grant said, and Rachael blinked at him. "I do computer-aided drafting and design for a construction company. Basically, I create technical schematics and blueprints for the crew to use."

"Interesting," Rachael said. "I want to hear more. From both of you."

The three of them discussed their careers as they polished off the rest of the food. Rachael tried to decline a second brownie, but it was impossible to deny hot men feeding her chocolate. They took turns, breaking off little bites for her to eat, and by the time the dessert was gone, she was a needy mess.

Reeve cleared away the dishes, and unable to wait another minute, Rachael ripped her shirt off and tackled Grant to the mattress.

"Hell yes! Time for round two," he said with a grin as he grabbed her hips.

"Round two?" Rachael giggled. "I think this is about round four. At least, if we're counting my orgasms."

Grant chuckled and nibbled at her breasts. "I am definitely counting your orgasms. My goal is to give you twice as many as you've ever had in one night before."

Rachael didn't have the heart to tell him he'd already done that. Besides, the last thing she wanted was to discourage him from continuing to try. Instead, she leaned in to kiss him.

The mattress sank beneath Reeve's weight as he settled on her other side. "Grant has the best ideas." He ran a hand up her leg.

Rachael laughed softly and continued kissing Grant. After a few minutes, Grant released her to kiss Reeve, licking and nipping and biting at his lower lip. Rachael squirmed on the bed, and Grant reached for her. She brought his hand to her chest, and he took her nipple between his fingertips and gently rolled it. Reeve's hand moved to Grant's hip to pull them all closer together. She found herself rocking against Grant's thigh, needing the friction against her pussy as she watched them kiss. Grant made a low sound in his throat and eventually pushed Reeve away.

"I think Rachael needs us to take care of her," he gasped.

Reeve grinned at the sight of her body molded to Grant's. "Mmm, I think she does. How about we get you ready to take both of us, Rachael?"

She shivered at the thought, and Reeve's face took on a thoughtful expression. "But only if you're sure that's what you want." he said.

She reached out to touch him. Reassure him. "I want it. The thought of both of you inside me turns me on so much."

"You've never been with two guys before, right?" he asked, and she shook her head.

"I have a toy that my ex used in me while he fucked me. It wasn't great, but that was mostly because he had a lousy rhythm."

Reeve smirked. "No worries there. Has it been a while?"

"Uh, yeah. A couple years, but I still play with the toy."

"Mmm." The groan that rumbled in Grant's chest made her press tighter against him. "I love picturing you playing like that. What kind of toy?"

"Uh, well, I have a small vibrator that I usually use first, then a bigger dildo."

"Grant's right," Reeve said. "Fuck. That's incredibly hot to think about. Rachael, what do you do when you get the bigger dildo inside of you?"

She bit her lip. "Play with my pussy."

Grant moved his hands to her hips, then dragged her over him so she lay directly on top. Reeve positioned himself between Grant's legs. Reeve's hands began to roam her legs softly at first.

"Did you ever put the vibrator in your pussy while the plug was in your ass?" Grant asked.

"A couple times." Rachael moaned when the pressure from Reeve's hands deepened.

"And what happens when you do?" Grant looked up at her, and his hands met Reeve's on the back of her thighs, pulling them apart so her knees fell onto the bed beside his hips, and she was spread open. She shivered at how vulnerable the position left her. And yet, she felt completely safe in their hands.

"I come so hard I see stars," she whispered.

Grant pulled her a bit higher on his body, and she settled on top of him again, her elbows on the bed beside his head. He drew her down until their lips met, and they kissed deeply while Reeve ran his hands along her lower back and over her ass. She felt him shift on the bed between Grant's thighs and kiss his way down her spine, his soft hair tickling her skin as his wet lips caressed her. Her breathing sped up as he reached the base of her spine. His thumbs gently pulled her cheeks apart before his tongue touched her back entrance. She gasped and squirmed on top of Grant, feeling the needy press of his cock against her inner thigh. Grant moved his lips to her neck, and she cried out softly when Reeve's tongue became more insistent. He traced a circle with his tongue, more and more firmly until she was panting and writhing on Grant, overwhelmed by the feeling.

"He's so good at that, isn't he?" Grant groaned roughly in her ear. "I can't believe how good that tongue feels on a sensitive place like that."

Grant's hand tangled in her hair as he bit lightly at her neck. Reeve worked his tongue a little deeper into her, pulling her hips up and back so he could access her better. She shuddered at the unbelievable sensations coursing through her body, all of her senses on overload.

Eventually, Reeve sat back and groaned. "Fuck, Rachael, your pussy is dripping all over Grant. You want this so bad, don't you?"

"Yes," she panted. She heard the quiet snick of a bottle being opened and a slick finger gently slipped between her cheeks. She pushed back, encouraging him. He rubbed tiny circles at first before gently putting pressure on her opening. His finger slid in with ease, and she felt him drizzle lube then add a second.

She was a little apprehensive, but fuck it, she *wanted* this. Grant helped her shift until her head rested against his shoulder, and he stroked her hair, soothing her as she did her best to relax when Reeve's fingers pushed into her.

"Tell me if you need me to back off," he whispered, delving the fingers of his other hand into her pussy to bring her even more pleasure.

"It's good," she said with a gasp. Reeve gave her body a moment to adjust before he began to work his fingers in and out of her again. She felt dizzy with pleasure, and she rocked unashamedly on top of Grant, who dragged his blunt fingernails up her back, sending little shudders of pleasure through her whole body.

After a few minutes of easy stroking, Reeve picked up the pace a little. "Are you ready for another finger?" he asked roughly, and she gasped, "Yes."

"Please, more," she begged.

Reeve's touch disappeared for a moment, then she felt the pressure as three fingers pushed gently into her ass. They were slick with lube, but the pressure still made her gasp, her eyes rolling back in her head at the thought of the way Reeve and Grant's cocks would fill her.

When her body had relaxed enough to easily accept Reeve's three fingers, he stilled. "You ready for a cock?" he asked.

"Yes. Please fuck me, both of you," she begged, half out of her mind with pleasure. They gently helped turn her over. Grant sat up against the headboard and pulled her back against his chest. Reeve prepared Grant's cock with a condom and a ridiculous amount of lube. Reeve steadied her so she hovered over Grant's cock, and Grant gently wound their legs together until she was open and ready. His cock nudged the entrance to her ass, and she took a deep breath, giving herself over to them. Trusting them to bring her pleasure.

Grant pushed against her, sliding into her ass with a pinch of discomfort before she remembered to relax. When Reeve moved a hand to her pussy, she panted with pleasure. She was slick with arousal, and the added stimulation helped her relax around Grant.

She whimpered when Reeve pulled away, but a few moments later, he touched her again, his fingers slippery with lube. She winced when he slid three fingers into her pussy, the fullness and pressure making her stomach clench. He was gentle, though, and his other hand rubbed her thigh, coaxing her to relax around the intrusion.

"Are you ready for me, sweet cheeks?" Reeve's voice was a low, rough growl as he used his fingers to spread her wider.

"Yes," Rachael panted. "I need you."

After he rolled a condom over his length, he leaned forward, bracing himself against the headboard. The head of his cock rubbed across her pussy lips at first, making her moan and clench around Grant. He gasped in her ear, then his hands moved to caress her nipples.

"Please, Reeve," she begged, and he aligned himself and pushed forward slowly. His gaze never left her face, and when she winced at the fullness, he paused, his jaw tight and strained. She took a few deep breaths, trying to relax. Grant was very still beneath her, and he moved his lips to her neck and dropped his hand to her clit, slowly stroking it.

"Keep going," she encouraged Reeve, and he slowly pushed forward again. She let her head fall back onto Grant's shoulder, and she panted, taking a moment to get used to the feeling of being that full. They very slowly began to rock, Reeve doing the majority of the thrusting.

The sensations were indescribable, and she lost herself in a daze after that. There were hands and lips and tongues and cocks on and in her, and she stopped trying to tell who was touching her where. Instead, she gave into the overwhelming pleasure. She gasped and writhed and moaned until she couldn't take any more. She cried out, the orgasm crashing over her in wave after wave of white-hot pleasure. She gripped them both tightly and felt them shudder against her, Grant coming just a moment before Reeve did. Pressed between their firm bodies, she let go, her throat growing raw from the sounds she made. The pleasure went on and on, so intense she could hardly catch her breath. The smallest of movements from either of them was enough to set her off again, and she felt completely delirious with pleasure, everything in the room going white and fuzzy as she struggled to breathe.

When Rachael came back to her senses, Grant and Reeve were both still inside her. She panted, trying to catch her breath. They murmured softly to her, and she finally realized they were asking her if she was all right.

"So good," she gasped.

Reeve gently pulled out, and she shuddered, her flesh over-sensitive to any touch. He soothed her, winding his fingers through hers, and she grasped them tightly when Grant pulled out. He was careful, but she winced anyway.

Her body was not only sensitive, but achy. They settled her on the bed, and Reeve removed the condom then curled around her. Grant appeared with a warm, damp cloth, and they took care of her, cleaning her and massaging her body as the pleasure slowly dissipated. Her muscles were weak and shaky, and her breathing was still shallow and ragged. Grant curled up on the other side of her, pulling the covers up over all of them, cocooning her in.

"Are you all right, gorgeous?" Grant asked softly, and she nodded vigorously.

"I feel amazing," she said with a contented sigh, her head swimming deliriously.

"Good." Reeve smiled at her. "You scared us for a minute."

"It was perfect," she slurred, her eyes already feeling heavy. Grant turned out the light beside the bed, and for a few minutes, they lay there silently in the dark, the only sound their deep breathing. Rachael rolled to her left, pressing her up against Grant. He sleepily pulled her close, and Reeve's arm came to rest across her waist so the three of them were sandwiched tightly together.

Still blissful from the pleasure they had brought her, Rachael closed her eyes. In moments, they were all sound asleep.

R achael woke sometime in the early morning. She was uncomfortably warm, and it took her a moment to realize why. Her deliciously aching body was a quick reminder when she tried to move. She was surrounded by and completely entwined with Reeve and Grant. She faced Reeve with her nose pressed against his chest. His right arm was thrown over her waist, and his left was under her pillow. Grant was tucked tight against her back, and when she sat up a little, she saw that his hands were loosely intertwined with Reeve's.

Reeve shifted on the bed. "Where are you going, beautiful?" His voice was gravely, even at a whisper.

"I'm too warm," Rachael quietly explained.

"Sorry."

Reeve untangled his fingers from Grant's and wrapped his arms around her waist and rolled so she was on the outside edge of the bed, and he was between her and Grant.

"Better?" he asked, brushing her hair off her face.

"Mmhmm."

Reeve settled on his side and spooned against her. He tucked her hair out of the way, and she tried not to melt at the sweet gesture.

"Are you okay otherwise? Not too sore?" he whispered in her ear.

"Achy and a little sore—" she admitted, "—but not bad. I don't mind."

He brushed his fingertips down her arm, raising goosebumps on her skin. "You sure? Things got a little wild there. I was afraid we hurt you."

"No, not at all," Rachael reassured him. "I feel great overall, really. I have no regrets."

"Good."

Reeve fell back to sleep almost immediately, but Rachael stayed awake, her mind too turbulent to rest. She wasn't used to sleeping in any bed but her own, or with anyone else in it, much less *two* someones. She certainly wasn't ashamed of going home with two virtual strangers. It had been the most incredible, earth-shattering pleasure she'd ever experienced. She'd felt safe and comfortable with them and didn't have a shred of regret about having a threesome with them. But she did wonder what came next. Rachael had absolutely no idea what expectations they had about what would happen this morning. Last night had been perfect, and the fact they'd wanted her to stay was nice. But what happened in the morning, and after?

If they wanted her again, should she go for it? She wanted to; there was no doubt about that. Despite the lingering aches in her body, it had been the most intense pleasure of her life. But was it really a good idea?

When Rachael realized she couldn't seem to slow down her brain, she crawled out from under Reeve's arm. She wasn't exactly feeling ready to bolt, but she knew she couldn't fall back asleep either, and she didn't want to disturb the guys. Rachael reached for the first shirt she ran across. As she slipped on the black T-shirt, Grant's cologne wafted toward her nose.

Rachael walked out into the living room. She stood by the window, looking out onto the dark, quiet street in front of the apartment, trying to process everything. If going home with a man she hardly knew was confusing, going home with two more than doubled the questions in her mind. Reeve had said that he and Grant weren't in a relationship, but what were they exactly? And how did she fit in?

After a while, she realized she was chilled. She stepped back from the window and grabbed a throw blanket off the back of a chair and wrapped herself in it. A few moments later, Reeve appeared in the doorway.

"Running away?" Reeve asked quietly.

Rachael shook her head and took a seat on the couch. "No. Just had some trouble sleeping."

Reeve settled his hip against the doorway, then relaxed against it. She stared at him, clad in nothing but a pair of boxers, remembering the way his naked body had felt against hers last night. "You okay?"

"I'm just not used to sleeping next to someone, much less two people. I woke up, then I couldn't fall back asleep."

"But you're okay physically?" he asked with a frown.

She smiled at him. "Oh, yeah. A little achy in some places, but overall, really, really good."

The worry in his voice was clear. "I was worried maybe we got too rough."

"No, Reeve, I'm fine, really; I promise."

"So it isn't regret keeping you up?"

"No. Definitely not," Rachael said firmly. "It was amazing. You fulfilled a fantasy I didn't know I had. Well, never thought I'd get to act on, anyway."

When Reeve continued to look at her steadily without saying a word, she tucked her feet under her and patted the couch beside her hip. She tried to pull together the thoughts in her head so she could explain to him what was going on. "I promise, I don't have any regrets about last night, Reeve."

"I'm very glad to hear that," Reeve said as he sat beside her. "I can honestly say it was the best threesome Grant and I have had."

"That's nice to hear," she admitted.

Reeve held out an arm to her, and she curled up against his side, pulling the blanket around them.

"Tell me about you and Grant," she said.

"What about us?"

"How you met, what you two are exactly."

Reeve chuckled. "Well, I can tell you how we met, but I'm afraid I can't tell you what we are. We've never really defined anything." He took a deep breath and continued. "I'm twenty-nine, and Grant is thirty-two. We met about three years ago, in a bar, actually."

Rachael smiled at the thought.

"I was playing a gig there—"

"You're a musician?" she interrupted. "On top of owning a music store?"

"Yeah, I play guitar and sing occasionally. That night, I was playing at Aces."

She recognized the name. It had been a crummy little bar across town that had closed about a year ago.

"So, you were playing when you saw Grant?" she asked.

"Yes. He kept sneaking side-long glances my way and downing beer. I'd been single for a while, and he caught my eye. So when my set was over, I wandered over to talk to him. He was a little hesitant; he'd just ended a relationship and was drinking to forget. But I sweet-talked him into coming home with me."

Rachael chuckled. It wasn't hard to imagine how Reeve had done that. He could talk the panties off a nun. She suspected both of them could. "You guys had sex?"

Reeve smiled. "We sure did."

"Who made the first move?"

"I don't really know. It was pretty mutual, I think. It was one of the hottest nights I'd experienced up to that point, though." Reeve got a faraway look on his face. "He fucked me over the kitchen table."

Rachael coughed. Picturing *that* sent a surge of heat through her.

"Did Grant spend the night?"

Reeve shook his head. "Nah, we ate sandwiches, then he headed home. And he didn't stay after the second time either. But after that, he sometimes did."

"Did you ever date?"

Reeve shook his head. "It's been really casual. We became friends, and we sure didn't try to deny the attraction, but we never defined anything. Sometimes, we hung out totally platonically. Sometimes, we couldn't keep our hands off each other. It's hard to explain, I guess. At this point, he's one of my best friends, he's my lover, but he's definitely not my boyfriend. I thought about it a few times, but he wasn't in a place where he wanted a serious relationship, and I was fine with it."

"That's interesting. So you dated other people throughout that time?" she asked.

"Yeah, quite a few."

"Men or women?"

"Mostly women, but a few men."

"What about Grant?"

For the first time, Reeve hesitated to answer her questions. "Well, that's more his story to tell than mine."

"Fair enough. So since then, you guys hook up occasionally? With or without a third person?"

"Both. The times with a third are relatively rare. Finding someone we're both attracted to, who is interested in both of us and accepting of the idea of Grant and I fucking, is surprisingly hard to come by."

"Do you *prefer* being with two people at once?" she asked.

"No, not necessarily. It does add a certain … intensity to the experience, though."

"So I noticed."

Reeve laughed softly. "You certainly seemed to be enjoying yourself."

"That's probably the understatement of the century."

"I'm glad. It's what we were hoping for."

"Of course, after a year and a half of celibacy, I desperately needed to get off," Rachael admitted.

"Are you saying that anyone else could have satisfied you that way?" he asked teasingly.

Rachael shook her head. "Not in the least. I imagine you and Grant are a rather unique experience."

"I like to think so."

"But you said you don't normally have people stay after."

"Yeah." Reeve tilted his head to look at her. "It's never been like *this*."

"I don't really know what that means," she admitted.

Reeve hesitated. "You know how sometimes you meet someone, and you think it'll just be a fun night in bed, but by the morning, you're trying to figure out how to get them to stay. And one night turns into a couple days and …"

"… and then you're dating that person, and you don't really know how it happened because it was never your plan," she finished. "Yeah, I've been there."

Reeve smiled faintly. "Well, that's where I'm at."

"Oh." Rachael had no idea how to respond.

Reeve stroked her hair, and Rachael tried to stifle an unexpected yawn.

"Sleepy?" Reeve asked.

"Yeah, I think I am," she admitted. "It just kinda snuck up on me."

"C'mere." Reeve pulled her up onto his chest with his arms wrapped tightly around her.

After they got comfortable, Rachael felt her earlier chaotic thoughts finally beginning to settle. She hadn't come to any conclusions about what she wanted, but at least, now she knew Reeve was feeling something similar to what she was. With her thoughts put to rest, she fell asleep quickly.

Hours later, she awoke to the smell of coffee. She snuggled deeper into the warm arms around her, then slowly opened her eyes. Grant stood in the kitchen, drinking coffee and smiling at Reeve and her. She blinked in surprise, and he grinned at her and motioned for her to join him. When she gently unwound herself from Reeve's arms, he sighed and rolled onto his left side. She covered him with one of the throws on the couch. The heat had obviously kicked on, and the apartment was warmer than it had been in the middle of the night, so she was comfortable in Grant's shirt.

Grant handed her a mug of coffee, and she followed him into the dining room. She curled her feet up onto the chair beneath her and savored the coffee for a moment before speaking.

"Sorry," she finally said in a quiet tone.

"For what?"

"Stealing Reeve from you last night."

"It's fine. Honestly. You two made an awfully pretty picture cuddled up there on the sofa." Grant chuckled. "It was just funny. I had a whole big bed to myself, and you two were crammed onto the couch."

"I couldn't sleep and came out here to think," Rachael admitted. "He came out a while later and we talked."

"Lemme guess, you had a few things you needed to work out in your head?"

"Yeah, I did."

"That's natural. Did Reeve help you straighten it out?"

"He helped." She clung to the mug like it was a life raft. "He's really easy to talk to."

"He is." Grant smiled. "That man ... he's definitely one-of-a-kind."

"So I'm gathering. Although, I think you both are, in your own ways."

"I suppose you're right." Grant gave her a speculative look over his coffee cup. "You're not like any woman I've ever met, either."

"Thanks. I hope that's a good thing."

"It's what made last night so goddamn good."

She shivered, remembering.

"So what has your thoughts in a snarl?"

"I don't know." Rachael sighed and drank more coffee. "It's not regret, or shame, or any of that. I don't have a problem with what we did last night. In fact, it was a really incredible experience."

"Well, I'm glad to hear that." Grant gave her a toothy smile, and she returned it. She still didn't know how to explain what was going on in her head, though. Maybe she could start with something a little easier—getting to know Grant.

"Reeve told me about how you met and a little about your dynamic. I guess I can't use the word relationship, can I?"

Grant shrugged. "It is a relationship, of sorts. But you're right, he's not my boyfriend, and I never really wanted him to be."

"Why do you think that is?" Rachael asked curiously.

"I don't know. I love him. I respect him. I can't imagine my life without him in it in some capacity. But when we met, I was just getting over a rough breakup, and the last thing I wanted was to get into something else. So Reeve and I settled into this great situation of being great friends who had amazing sex. It never really felt right to pursue something more serious."

"Hmm, that's interesting."

"It is," Grant agreed. "And no matter how many times I've thought about it, I've always reached the same conclusion. I don't know; it just felt like something was missing between Reeve and me. Not in a bad way; it just didn't feel right. Then again, I've never been much of one for monogamy anyway."

"Why is that?"

"I don't know. I know it's good for a lot of people. And I respect couples who find each other and make it work. But I always feel like something's missing. Now Reeve, he's a bit more comfortable with it than I've been."

"Really?" Rachael said, surprised to hear that.

"Really. That being said, he's not a possessive man, and he wants his own freedom. I don't know that he'd want to give up what he and I have any more than I do."

Rachael drained the rest of her coffee and looked at Grant speculatively, trying to sort through everything in her head. She was still trying to understand both Grant and Reeve better and had a few questions. "You don't see yourself in a monogamous relationship then? Not ever?"

"For a while, there was a beautiful, amazing woman I was seein'. Her name was April. She was smart and strong and like no one else. But, she had a rough time when she was younger. She married someone who treated her awfully, emotionally abused her, and made her feel caged in. She's moved past it, healed, but she's never going to want a ring on her finger and some signature on a piece of paper. She loved me, and I loved her. It was as simple as that."

Rachael furrowed her brow. "Wait, I don't understand. What does that have to do with you and Reeve?"

Grant leaned forward. "She was the one who introduced me to the idea of polyamory."

Rachael felt foolish. "That's the idea of loving more than one person, right?"

"In essence."

"So she was totally okay with you and Reeve?"

"I ended things with her before I met Reeve." His expression turned wistful. "She was the person I was trying to get over the night I met Reeve, actually."

"Oh."

"But I did date other people while I was with her."

"Did she join you with any of those people?"

He shook his head. "No, it wasn't something she was interested in. It fell outside of her comfort zone. But she didn't begrudge it to me. And she went home with a guy occasionally when she felt like it. It worked for us. I don't know that it would have worked for many other couples, but it did for us."

"It didn't bother you to know she was with another man?"

Grant shook his head. "No. April taught me love doesn't have to be limiting. It should only expand who you are and make you feel free."

"I'm not trying to be judgmental."

"I know you aren't. It's honest curiosity, and I respect that." Grant lifted his coffee cup to his lips. When he lowered it, he continued. "When April touched another man, it didn't mean she loved me any less. Like I said, I know it's not for everyone, but she opened up a whole new world to me. I haven't looked back since."

"Why did things end with her?" Rachael asked.

Grant sighed heavily. "I couldn't give her what she wanted." Sorrow flickered over his face, but he didn't continue. There was obviously more to the story, but it was equally clear that Grant didn't want to discuss it.

"I'm sorry," Rachael said quietly.

Grant waved off her apology. "However things ended between us, she taught me a lot. I'll always be grateful for that. What about you? Any interesting stories to tell about your past, Rachael?"

"I'm all for getting to know each other better"—a voice behind Rachael said—"but I'm starving. Do you think we can do it over brunch?"

Reeve's arms were braced on either side of the doorframe, and his shirtless state made it very easy for Rachael's gaze to traverse his upper body. His shoulders were so broad, and his stance emphasized his biceps and pecs. Every muscle was finely honed and lean.

"Christ, *he* looks good enough to eat, doesn't he?" Grant murmured lowly.

Reeve's crooked smirk told Rachael that he heard Grant, despite the quiet tone. "I'm up for heading back into the bedroom *after* brunch."

Rachael grinned at Reeve as he crossed the room to them. "It seems like you both need to be fed often."

He laughed, looking down at her as he rubbed her shoulders. "Hey, we expended some major energy last night."

Rachael smiled, remembering. "That we did."

"So, what now?" Reeve asked, letting go of her shoulders. "You don't have to work today, right?"

"I don't have anything planned," she admitted. That reminded her; she needed to text Jenna and let her know how the night had gone.

"Then how about we hop in the shower, then go out to brunch. Get to know each other," Reeve suggested as he moved to stand in front of her. He held out a hand to pull her to her feet.

"I'd like that." Rachael stood, and Grant nodded his agreement and followed suit.

He reached out, wrapping an arm around Rachael's waist to draw her closer. "You know, it just occurred to me that we were never properly introduced. I don't even know your last name."

Rachael shook her head and giggled at the thought of all that had happened in the last twelve hours.

"Rachael Bradford."

"Grant McGuire; pleased to make your acquaintance." Grant grinned at her, his eyes sparkling as he lifted her hand to his mouth. Grant kissed her hand and passed her over to Reeve.

He smiled down at her. "I'm still going to call you sweet cheeks, but it's very nice to officially meet you, Rachael Bradford."

"You too," she barely managed to reply before he leaned down and kissed her. It was thorough, lingering, and when he pulled back, she felt flushed and breathless. Reeve didn't let go when he pulled back, but he did shift to the side to make room for Grant. When Reeve and Grant kissed, Rachael unabashedly stared at them until they separated.

"I hope your shower is big enough for three," Rachael said.

Reeve smiled. "I think I can make room for both of you."

"Oh, my God, that was amazing," Rachael said, pushing her nearly empty plate away from her. She had devoured several slices of French toast stuffed with cream cheese and topped with mixed berries, not to mention bacon, orange juice, and coffee. Apparently, the guys weren't the only ones who had expended a lot of energy.

"Told you." Reeve smirked at her. "Best breakfast in town."

Grant glanced at his phone. "Even if we are eating it at three in the afternoon. Gotta love diners that serve breakfast all day."

Reeve chuckled and leaned in, speaking low enough that only Grant and Rachael could hear him. "You were the one who fingered Rachael in the shower."

Grant shrugged. "And you were the one who gave me a handjob. So, I guess we're all to blame."

90

She laughed. It had been a very enjoyable—if snug—shower together. "Hey, what did I do? I was innocently showering, and you two couldn't keep your hands to yourselves."

Reeve gave her a disbelieving look. "You were all naked. And soapy. And looking like *that*."

She glanced down at herself. She wore the clothes from the night before. Her hair was pulled up in a messy bun and was still damp from the shower, and she didn't have on a speck of makeup except the lip gloss she'd had in her purse and had probably eaten off by now. She was probably a hot mess right now, but she sure couldn't tell from the way Reeve and Grant looked at her. At least, Reeve had loaned her a toothbrush and a pair of boxer briefs. He'd threatened to keep her panties as collateral until Grant had ended the argument by swearing he'd leave for brunch without them.

Reeve sprawled in his seat, his booted feet bumping Rachael's. "I am so full." He patted his flat stomach, looking entirely fuckable in a pair of dark jeans and a snug, white long sleeve T-shirt.

"That's because you ate like you'd never get fed again," Grant said, elbowing Reeve in the ribs. Grant had borrowed a gray sweater that was a hair too short and a pair of Reeve's underwear. He exchanged a smile with Rachael, and she had to stifle a sigh. God, they were both incredibly gorgeous. And they were so easy to talk to. Their conversations over brunch ranged across a wide variety of topics, and she'd laughed more in an hour than she had in the past few months.

"You ready to go, sweet cheeks?" Rachael looked up at Reeve and realized he had stood. Grant was up near the register, paying for their breakfasts. She'd been so wrapped up in her thoughts she hadn't noticed.

"Oh, yeah. Sorry." She stood, and Reeve grabbed her jacket before she could, holding it up for her. Flustered, she allowed him to help her into it. When was the last time a guy had been so chivalrous?

They met Grant at the register. He tucked a receipt into his wallet and fell into step beside them. Grant held the door while Reeve guided her toward the parking lot with a hand on her back. They'd all ridden together in Reeve's car, and he opened the door to let her in.

She'd never felt like she *needed* a man to take care of her, but there was something sweet and wonderful about the way both Grant and Reeve treated her. It was a novel experience.

They were halfway back to the apartment when Reeve caught her glance in the rearview mirror. "You still back there, sweet cheeks? You're awfully quiet."

"I'm fine. Just in a food coma." She smiled at him. "And thinking about you two."

"What about us?" He waggled his eyebrows in the rearview mirror. "Dirty things, I hope."

She chuckled. "Actually, I was thinking that you two are some of the nicest guys I've ever met. Incredible in bed, yes. But also some of the most thoughtful. It was nice getting to know the other side of you at brunch."

"Do you want to come back up to the apartment when we get back?" he said as he turned off the main road.

"Going to bed with you two again wouldn't be a hardship, but I could probably use a break," she admitted.

Grant turned in his seat to look back at her. "You okay?"

"Absolutely." She gave him a reassuring smile. "I'm just a little sore from all the orgasms. Not bad sore, but *more* sex would probably be pretty uncomfortable."

"We *are* capable of restraining ourselves," Reeve said. "I'd be totally fine with just hanging out and watching a movie or something."

Rachael hesitated. "Honestly, I'd kinda like to go home. I'm wearing the clothes I worked in yesterday, and I do have some stuff to do around the house today. I'd put it off, but I have to go to the bar tomorrow to get some work done."

Truthfully, she needed some time to think too. Her time with the guys had been amazing, but she was suddenly inundated with doubt. The nagging question of "what happened now?" wouldn't go away.

"Okay." Reeve sounded a little disappointed, but he pulled into the empty parking spot next to her car. He and Grant both got out, and Rachael followed more slowly.

"Thanks for brunch." She tried to smile normally, but Grant was the one who spotted her turmoil. "Are you okay?" He gently touched her elbow.

"I just … I don't know what happens after this morning. Is this 'goodbye' or 'I'll see you again'?"

Reeve exchanged a glance with Grant, then frowned at her. "What do *you* want?"

"I … I don't know," she admitted. She looked between them. She couldn't imagine walking away and never seeing either of them ever again, but she still didn't have a clue what she did want.

"You don't have to have all of the answers now," Reeve said gently. "Take your time; think it over. But I can honestly say I'd be very disappointed if I didn't see you again."

She turned to Grant. "What about you?"

He smiled at her and skimmed his thumb across her cheekbone. "I'd be disappointed as well."

"So the three of us are going to … what?" she asked. "Get together occasionally for hookups?"

"If that's what you'd like," Grant said.

"I don't know what I want," Rachael admitted. "I've never been in a situation like this before. I don't even know what my options are."

Grant chuckled. "Fair enough. The 'where do we go from here?' issue can be a tricky one. Reeve and I sure mulled that one over ourselves several times, that's for sure."

Reeve let out a sigh. "Can we stop being so polite about all of this and actually be clear? Look, I meant what I said. You don't have to decide *anything* right now, Rachael. Let's exchange numbers, you and me, and you and Grant. And let's get together again in a couple days. It can be a wild night in bed again, or we can sit down and have dinner and see if maybe the three of us have something *outside* of the bedroom too. I know I'm not the only one thinking the potential's there."

Rachael shook her head. "You're not the only one thinking that. I just wasn't sure what you guys were looking for." At first, she'd felt like she was being presumptuous, assuming they'd want something more than a one-night stand. And that they would want it with her. But it was pretty clear she'd been wrong about that.

Reeve shrugged. "I'm not *looking* for anything. But if an amazing opportunity like this drops in my lap, I'm willing to give it a shot. I like you, Rachael. I'd like to know you better. I know I like Grant and want him in my life. Does it have to be more complicated than that?"

"Sometimes you oversimplify things, Reeve," Grant said, but there was no harshness to his tone. Just a quiet resignation like they'd had that conversation a thousand times before. He looked at Rachael. "I do agree with Reeve, though. I'd like to get to know you better and see what happens. I'm not ruling anything out."

"Okay. I'm good with that," she agreed. "Why don't we have dinner in a couple days and see what happens then?"

Reeve's face lit up with a smile. "I like the sound of that." He leaned forward and kissed her soundly. Grant's reaction was a little more subdued but no less heartfelt. They exchanged numbers, and Grant held her car door open for her as Reeve scraped the frost off the windows.

Before he shut the door, Grant leaned in. She glanced up at him quizzically.

"Think about all the possible options for the next few days," he said. "Reeve and I, we both like you a lot, but this can be whatever the three of us make it. There are no limitations."

R achael drummed her short fingernails on the kitchen table as she waited for someone to pick up the phone at the bar.

"Hawk Point Tavern, how can I help you?"

"Jenna? It's Rach."

"Hey! I was starting to wonder if the hotties had actually kidnapped and murdered you." Rachael heard Jenna cover the phone, then a muffled, "Hey, Tyler, I'm taking my break now. Cover me?" before she continued. "I'm going into your office so we can talk."

"Actually," Rachael said, "would you come over to my place after your shift? I kinda want to talk in person. Unless you and Karl have plans."

"Nah, he's going to play pool with some of the guys from the shop tonight," Jenna said. "I'll be happy to come over. Is everything okay?" Her tone turned serious. "Nothing sketchy happened right?"

"Oh, God, no," Rachael reassured her. "I'm fine. I had an amazing time, honestly. I'll go into details later, but I guess they—*we*—are all considering seeing each other again, and I'm kinda conflicted. I could use your advice."

"You had me worried there! But I'm glad it went well, and I'll be happy to talk. I'll be over as soon as my shift is over."

"Thanks, Jenna."

"Anything for you, boss lady," Jenna said, and Rachael smiled at the nickname.

After she hung up, Rachael spent the rest of the afternoon and evening puttering around the house. She did laundry and cleaned the bathroom before curling up on the couch with a book. It did nothing to distract her, though, and she found herself re-reading the same page multiple times. The knock on the door was a relief.

Jenna had taken her long blonde hair down from the ponytail she usually wore it up in while she worked but was still dressed in her work uniform and carrying a bag emblazoned with the nearby Mexican restaurant's logo. "I brought dinner. Hopefully, you didn't eat already."

"No, I had a late brunch," Rachael admitted. "I hadn't even thought about dinner. Thanks. C'mon in."

Once they'd unpacked the food and taken a seat in the kitchen, Jenna stared at her from the other side of the table. "Okay, *spill*, woman."

"I don't even know where to start," Rachael said with a soft laugh as she filled her plate with chicken nachos.

"How was it?"

"Amazing."

"I'd like more than one-word answers, please," Jenna begged. "I need to live vicariously through you. You have no idea how much that's always been a fantasy of mine."

"Really?"

"Uh, yeah. Two men lavishing all their attention on me sounds fabulous."

Rachael laughed as she scooped guacamole onto her plate. "Well, I wasn't the only one in the middle, so to speak. Although, that part was definitely incredible."

"God, I bet. Did they both fuck you at once? DP?"

Rachael laughed softly and dumped sour cream on her nachos. "Yes."

"Damn," Jenna said, sounding impressed. She leaned forward to high five Rachael, who humored her and met her halfway. "You go, girl. How sore are you today?"

"I'm not going to be running a marathon or anything, but I'm *fine*. I had a hot shower and a couple aspirin earlier, and I feel great. Honestly, the sore muscles hurt worse than my ass."

Jenna chuckled. "Well, good. Clearly, they know what they're doing. God, I have to ask. How many orgasms did you have?"

Rachael thought for a moment then shrugged. "Six? No, eight? Maybe? It's kinda hazy. There was some tequila involved to get things rolling, and it's just a beautiful, delicious blur after that. I mean, I *remember* it all, but I kind of lost track of the orgasms after a while."

"Son of a bitch," Jenna huffed. "Jealous. There's no other word for it."

"So ask Karl if he'll have one."

"Yeah, but he's straight, and it just wouldn't be the same," she whined. "I should have had you film last night."

"Jenna, I'm not making porn so you can watch it. That would just be weird. I'm your *boss*. Your best friend, but also your boss."

"You are no fun."

"And you're a perv."

"When have I ever denied that?" she asked incredulously. "Anyway, I'm very happy for you. I had a feeling they'd be pretty good in bed."

Rachael snorted and dug into her nachos. "Pretty good is an understatement. The sex was off the charts. Individually, either of them would have been amazing, but together … unreal."

Jenna frowned. "So what's the problem? You said you were conflicted about seeing them again. Why the hell not? I would be all over that!"

"Because I have no idea what I'm doing!" Rachael said. "I've never done this before."

"Done what?"

"This." Rachael gestured wildly. "Gotten involved with two guys at once! I mean, I've casually dated multiple people at a time, but I wasn't necessarily sleeping with all of them. And I sure as hell wasn't fucking several at *once*."

"Fucking two amazing men on a regular basis sounds like the complete opposite of a problem to me," Jenna said.

Rachael laughed. "I'm not saying sex with them is a problem." She hesitated. "But Reeve kinda sounds like he's interested in *more*. And Grant said he was open to the idea as well."

"More meaning what?"

"That's just it. I don't really know," Rachael admitted.

"I'm not sure I really get what those guys have going on," Jenna said.

"Me either. I'm not sure *they* get it. They said they've been involved for a few years, but it's never been anything serious. Although, Grant said he loved Reeve. I think. Fuck, I don't know."

"Okay," Jenna said. "So let's break this down. Grant and Reeve are in some weird quasi-relationship but see other people, right?"

"Yes."

"And they both like you?" Rachael nodded. "And you like both of them?"

"Yeah."

"Do you like either of them better than the other?"

Rachael thought about it for a few long moments as she ate a few bites of her nachos, then shook her head. "No. I don't think so. It's really easy with Reeve. He and I seem to click really well. There was just that instant chemistry, but the more I talked to Grant, the more I liked him too."

"Okay. And what did you all decide before you left today?"

Rachael shrugged. "We're going to have dinner in a couple days. Grant suggested I think about what I wanted." She repeated what he'd said to her in the parking lot. "But I don't even know what the possibilities *are*."

"Well, one possibility is that you pick one or the other—which seems like something you would have a hard time doing."

"I can't imagine choosing between the two. And I feel like it would make things weird between them."

"Well, that's their responsibility, not *yours*," Jenna said. "But I get that. You don't want to pick."

"No, I don't."

"So then the option is that you fuck both of them—separately or together."

Rachael wrinkled her nose. "I think I'd prefer together. I mean, I'm not saying I'd never want one of them solo, but it seems less complicated if we're all together at once, right? Less chance of someone feeling neglected or ignored."

"Not to mention more fun." Jenna winked before turning serious again. "So is that all you want? Some great kinky sex?"

Rachael nibbled at a tortilla chip as she thought. "I don't think that's *all* I want. But how would that work?"

"What, dating both of them?"

"Yeah."

Jenna shrugged. "However you want."

"Ugh." Rachael pushed away her plate of food. "That doesn't help! That's what the guys both basically said."

"I know this is something totally new to you, Rach, but I think they're right. You could have any kind of relationship you want." Jenna frowned at her. "You're usually way more decisive, lady. This isn't like you at all. What's up?"

Rachael chewed at her lip. "Maybe I'm kinda leery because of the bi thing and my history with Tom. And Jonah."

"Well, I don't think you can really equate the two. Jonah was a cheating asshole. And Tom just didn't know he liked pussy *and* dick."

Rachael snorted. "I know. But it makes me kinda wary about getting involved with two bi guys."

"I don't see why. Reeve and Grant are clearly totally comfortable with their sexuality. They've already figured it out. That should actually be a selling point in their favor."

Rachael considered that. "Fair point."

"And as for Jonah, yeah, he was a liar and a cheater. Do your guys seem untrustworthy?"

Her guys? Hardly. But maybe a part of her wanted them to be. "No. They were nothing but trustworthy last night and this morning," she admitted. "And they've been really open about things. Grant was totally upfront about not being monogamous."

"Okay, so scratch everything we've just talked about." Jenna waved her hands. "Forget all of this speculation, and tell me one thing. If you could have anything you wanted, what would it be? Don't think about whether they would be okay with it or how you'd make it work. You can worry about that later. Just close your eyes and picture the perfect scenario of you with Reeve and Grant. What would it look like to you?"

Feeling silly, Rachael closed her eyes and let her mind wander. Various scenarios flitted through her head until she landed on one. It made her smile, and she opened her eyes. "The three of us dating," she admitted. "Not separately, but all together. Like a trio, I guess. All of us involved equally at the same time. But, I don't know that I can get involved with them while they're seeing other people."

Jenna grinned at her. "Well, there you go!"

"That's assuming they want that!" Rachael argued. "And that they'd be cool with dating me and each other and not seeing anyone *else*."

"There's only one way to find out," Jenna said philosophically as she scooped guacamole onto her tortilla chip. "Ask them."

Rachael's phone buzzed on the coffee table about an hour after Jenna left. She saw a text notification and a message from Reeve. *Hey, sweet cheeks.*

Hey, how's your night going? she replied, unable to stop the smile that crossed her face.

Pretty uneventful. Watching a movie.

Same here. Well, a TV show. Never seen it before but there's a spunky medical examiner solving cases.

Sounds fun. Reeve replied. And a moment later, another message popped up. *It would be more fun watching it together.*

Definitely. She chewed at her lip. *Thanks for last night. It was all kinds of amazing.*

No need to thank me. Thanks for trusting us enough to give it a shot.

I'm glad I did.

They texted back and forth about inconsequential things for a while, and Rachael found herself paying far more attention to the conversation than the show she was watching. When it was over, she shut off the TV and wandered through the house, turning off lights and checking the doors. It wasn't that late, but she hadn't gotten a ton of sleep the night before.

She fired off a quick message to Reeve. *Brushing my teeth, brb.*

She was in the middle of scrubbing when her phone vibrated on the bathroom counter. *Impatient much, Reeve?* she thought, smiling around her toothbrush, but it was a notification from Grant.

Hey there, gorgeous. I wanted to give you a little space today, but I wanted to let you know I was thinking about you.

She smiled wider, then had to wipe off the toothpaste that dribbled down her chin. She set down her phone and hastily finished her nightly routine. She typed a message back to Grant as she turned out the light in her bathroom and wandered into the bedroom.

Thanks! I've been thinking about you too.

Good things, I hope.

Most definitely.

Her phone buzzed with a message from Reeve. *How many teeth do you have???*

LOL, Grant messaged me. I got distracted, she answered.

Oh. Well, talking to Grant is always an acceptable excuse. He IS very distracting.

Then a message from Grant. *How was your day?*

Rachael laughed softly to herself. It took a few minutes to get used to having two simultaneous text conversations, but she eventually got the hang of it as she talked to Reeve and Grant about her day. A yawn caught her by surprise, and she blinked sleepily at the clock as she realized she could hardly keep her eyes open anymore.

A group chat message popped up before she could tell them she needed to head to bed.

Reeve: *My bed is feeling awfully big tonight without you two in it.*

Rachael: *It was cozy, but I got too warm in the middle!*

Grant: *I don't know what either of you are talking about since you abandoned me to spend half the night on the couch.*

Reeve: *Note to self: put Rachael on the outside next time. Does that mean I get the middle?*waggles eyebrows**

Grant: *Jesus, Reeve, don't be so pushy. We have to respect that maybe Rachael doesn't want another night with us.*

Reeve: *What? That's not possible, Grant. We're way too charming and good in bed to turn down. :)*

Rachael laughed aloud then read the message that popped up a moment later.

Reeve: *No. I'm kidding, Rachael. We totally respect that you might not want to continue. This is in your hands.*

Rachael thought for a moment before she typed her reply.

Rachael: *I definitely would like to see you guys again. I just need to sleep on it and be sure I know exactly what I want before we talk.*

Grant: *Take as much time as you need to think about it. We're not going anywhere.*

Rachael thanked them, explained how tired she was, and said goodnight.

After they responded, she set her phone to silent and plugged it in to charge for the night.

She fell asleep with a smile on her face.

She woke up to find a *Morning, gorgeous* message from Grant on her phone, and she replied before she got out of bed. She was sipping coffee at the kitchen table and checking her email when her phone pinged with a group text notification from Reeve. It was a picture of Reeve in bed, looking rumpled and entirely fuckable.

Woke up this morning thinking about you two. Going to take care of it in the shower.

Rachael laughed and told him to have fun.

Over a bowl of yogurt and granola, she thought more about her conversation with Jenna the previous day and how much she'd been enjoying chatting with Reeve and Grant.

You've found two incredible men who are both attracted to you and to each other. What are you so afraid of, Rachael? she asked herself.

"Everything," she whispered to the empty house. "This is huge. It's not something I can just jump into without thinking it through."

The nagging voice in her head that sounded an awful lot like Jenna answered. *What if you over-think this and end up missing out on an incredible opportunity?*

A surge of determination went through her, and before she could second-guess herself, she sent them a message in the group text.

If you're free, do you guys want to do dinner tonight and talk?

She got replies almost immediately.

Grant: *Works for me*

Reeve: *I'm there! Well, I'll be there once we decide where there is.*

Reeve's ability to be lighthearted about this made her smile.

Rachael: *LOL. My place? 6ish?*

Grant: *Sounds good. We'll take care of the food*

Rachael: *Hoping to win me over with your cooking? Reeve did chop a mean cheese cube the other night.*

Grant: *Well, I'm not above trying …*

Reeve: *Nah, I was going to use my skill at shoulder rubs and … other things.*

Rachael: *It might just work! ;) Okay, time for me to go, boys. I have to put in a few hours at the bar.*

She added her address on the end and sent a smiley face blowing a kiss, feeling silly and happy as she tried to ignore the flutter of nerves in her stomach.

A s Rachael opened the door at 5:58 that evening, the flutter of nerves had grown into a stampede. Expecting to see just one of them, she was surprised to see both Reeve and Grant on her doorstep.

"Hey, come in." She held the door open and gestured for them to come inside.

Reeve stepped in first. "Looking good, sweet cheeks." He leaned in to give her a fleeting but warm kiss on the lips. She'd dressed in her most flattering pair of jeans and a soft blue sweater and taken a little extra time on her hair and makeup.

Grant followed Reeve inside, smiling at Rachael over the bouquet of red tulips he held. "Hey there, gorgeous." He held the plastic wrapped bundle out.

"You got me flowers?" She took them with a smile.

"We did. I suggested them; Reeve picked them out." Grant tasted her lips briefly.

"It's freezing out there!" Reeve said. "Stop making out and shut the door."

Rachael had totally forgotten she still had the door open. "Sorry," she said with a laugh. She started to close the door but caught a glimpse of Mrs. Russell, the nosy old lady across the street. She stood by her car, staring at them. Whoops. Apparently, the whole neighborhood would find out that Rachael was involved with two men. She stifled a sigh, more resigned than upset by the idea. "Hi there, Mrs. Russell!" she called out and waved before she shut the door.

Grant raised an eyebrow at her. "Nosy neighbors?"

"The nosiest." Rachael shook her head. "Don't worry about it. I don't care. They already look at me funny when I blast death metal while I weed the flowerbeds."

"You listen to death metal?" Reeve gave her an intrigued look. "And is that Nina Simone I hear playing?"

"It is." She patted his hip as she walked past him. "I listen to a little bit of everything."

Reeve grinned widely at her. "I'm intrigued, woman."

"Feel free to hang up your coats on the rack there." She pointed at the wooden coatrack by the door and then toward the back of the house. "And then the kitchen is this way."

Once their coats were off, they followed her into the kitchen, and Reeve set two grocery bags on the small round table. "This is a great house, Rachael."

"Oh, thanks." She smiled at him and carefully propped the flowers up in the sink. It *was* a great house. It was a small bungalow built in the 40s, cozy but charming. "It belonged to my grandma. My mom inherited it from her. She rented it out for a while, but once my parents died, I decided to move in. I just couldn't live in the house where I'd grown up, so I sold it and put the money into fixing this place up. It's a nice connection to my family without being overwhelmed by the memories."

Her breath caught at the end, and Grant rubbed her back. "I totally understand that."

Not wanting to bring down the mood with her depressing history, she cleared her throat and pointed to the vases on top of the cabinet. "Reeve? Could you grab me one of those?"

He could easily reach the top. She had to stand on a chair to get them down. Well, *there* was a major advantage of having a couple tall guys around. "Of course. Which one?"

"Hmm, the white one, I think."

When the flowers were arranged and set on the table, she smiled at the guys. "Thank you. That was a nice surprise."

"Hey, we're not just good in the sack," Reeve said. His tone was defensive, but there was a twinkle in his eye as he reached into one of the bags and pulled out a head of lettuce.

"And you cook, apparently," she teased.

Grant crossed the small kitchen and helped Reeve unpack the groceries.

"We do." Grant looked up at her with a package of steaks in his hand. "That reminds me. Do you have a grill? If not, I can use your broiler, but grilling is so much better."

"I do." She pointed to the door on the other side of the kitchen. "Through the laundry room there. If you go through the door in the back, there's a little patio. The grill's covered right now, and the propane tank is in the garage, but you're welcome to use it if you'd like. You'll freeze out there, though."

Grant shrugged. "Once I get the grill going, I'll be fine. Is your garage unlocked?"

"Maybe? I'll run out with you and check."

"I'll get the steaks marinating and start the sides," Reeve said. "Mind if I take over your kitchen, sweet cheeks?"

She snorted. "Be my guest. I'll never turn down a hot man in my kitchen."

Reeve grinned at her, his eyes twinkling. "Duly noted."

Rachael led Grant out onto the patio, and he glanced around her tiny backyard. It was about the size of a postage stamp, but she had a few flowers she managed not to kill and enough room to have a few friends over for dinner in nice weather. The garage was detached from the house, and she tested the knob of the side door and found it locked. "Good thing I came out." She reached up, fishing blindly for the key holder attached to the base of the light fixture beside the door. Her sweater slid up, exposing her bare skin, and the cool air made her shiver. "Ah ha!" She pulled out the magnetic case and slid it open before dumping the spare key in her palm.

"You didn't see that," she threw over her shoulder at Grant. Not that she was actually worried about Grant breaking into her house, but she enjoyed teasing him.

He grinned. "I saw nothing. I swear."

Rachael was shivering by the time Grant fetched the propane tank, and he urged her to go inside. "Go in where it's warm, gorgeous. I'm all set."

He wore a thick off-white wool sweater, and her teeth were beginning to chatter, so she didn't argue. She gave him a brief kiss and fled for the warm house. Reeve was busy massaging herbs into the steaks, and he gave her a curious glance as she walked through the kitchen, but he didn't comment when she returned with Grant's jacket.

Grant took the black wool pea coat from her with a grateful smile and shrugged it on. "Thanks. Quick kiss before you leave?"

"Happily."

He tucked her against his chest and wrapped the coat around her. The kiss wasn't particularly quick, but it did leave her breathless when she finally drew back. And this time, the shivers that ran through her body had nothing to do with the cold.

"Give Reeve a kiss for me while I get the grill going. I'll be in shortly."

"I can do that!"

The house felt warm and cozy after the cold air outside. Reeve looked up from the vegetables he'd been chopping and smiled. "I thought maybe you were going to stay out with Grant."

"Nope." She stretched up and kissed him. "That's from him, though."

"Mmm. Nice message." He wrapped an arm around her waist and kissed her again. "And that's from me."

She smoothed her hand over the gray button-down he wore with the sleeves rolled up. "I could get used to this," she admitted.

Reeve raised an eyebrow at her. "Kissing me?"

"Kissing you and Grant. Having the two of you around my house," she admitted.

Reeve let out a little huff of frustration. "I *really* want to have that conversation with you, but I guess we should wait until Grant gets back."

"Yes." She stepped back before she got lost in him. "Can I help with dinner?"

"Well, you can find a bowl to put salad in. I wasn't sure what you usually used."

"Got it." She retrieved the bowl from a cabinet and reached for the lettuce that was drip-drying in a colander in her sink.

"Can I ask you some questions while we get dinner ready?" Rachael asked.

Reeve sounded surprised. "You can ask me anything. I'm an open book."

"How long have you known you were bi?"

Reeve shrugged and resumed chopping cucumber. "Seems like forever. I'd say high school was when I first really thought about it. I was dating a girl named Kristy at the time. She was a really sweet girl, fun and smart and all the things a high school girlfriend should be. We were happy together. But I realized I was checking out our friend Adam just as often. It didn't really make me uncomfortable, but I definitely wasn't sure how to handle it."

"I would imagine." She ripped the lettuce into pieces, dropping them in the bowl.

"I'll give Kristy this, she was pretty open-minded. When I admitted to her that I wasn't sure I was totally straight, she was more curious than anything else. And a few times, I caught her watching Adam and me when we were hanging out. After senior prom, the three of us ended up in a hotel room together. We were drunk but not out of control, just enough to lower the inhibitions. She watched while I sucked Adam off, then I fucked her. She gave him a handjob."

"Was it weird after?"

He chuckled. "You could say that. Adam was less comfortable with the idea of what we'd done than I was, and there were some lingering feelings between him and Kristy. But, honestly, we were seventeen. What did we think was going to happen? That's probably a bit young for anyone to be exploring the idea of multiple partners. The maturity just isn't there."

108

"True. Did you and Kristy stay together?"

"For a while. A few months, I think. And then she admitted her feelings for Adam. I won't say it ended well. There were a lot of hurt feelings on all sides, but it worked out for the best. Last I heard, they were still together."

"Oh, wow." Rachael heard the back door open and shut, and a few moments later, Grant appeared in the kitchen.

"No fighting fate, right?" Reeve chuckled. "After high school, I dated men and women. Personally, I found there to be very little difference. I liked who I liked, and the relationships had the same positive and negative aspects, no matter which gender I was dating."

"Were you out to your family?"

"Yeah, absolutely. And they were fine with it."

"You're lucky," Grant said, leaning against the counter between Rachael and Reeve.

Reeve set down his knife and reached out to touch Grant's arm. "I know I am. I tell myself that every day."

Grant looked down but not before Rachael saw the flicker of sorrow flash across his face. She reached out, and he willingly took her hand, winding their fingers together. "Thank you, gorgeous. I'm all right." He cleared his throat. "I was in college when I finally admitted to myself that I was attracted to men. I'd known for a long time, but knowing and admitting are two very different things. I knew I was still interested in women, but somehow, it seemed like that was almost worse than just being gay."

"Worse? Why?"

"I had more than one not-so-nice person tell me I was being greedy. That I should just pick one or the other. Being gay wasn't great, but it was excusable. It was an innate thing that couldn't be changed. But being bi meant I just wasn't choosing right."

Rachael squeezed his fingers.

"You have to understand, I came from a very Southern, very religious family. Conservative as all hell. A gay son, or a bi son, wasn't what they wanted. When I went to tell my family, I just told them I was gay. It seemed easier."

"How bad was it?"

"Bad. My father nearly had a heart attack screaming at me. He actually ended up in the hospital with chest pains."

"Oh, shit," she muttered, and Grant chuckled sadly.

"Yeah. He banned me from his hospital room, too. That was ten years ago, and I haven't spoken to him since."

"I'm so sorry," Rachael whispered. "That sounds awful."

"Thank you. It was."

"What about your mother?"

He sighed. "That's more complicated. She still loves me. She doesn't support my 'choice,' but she hasn't cut me out of her life completely. She sends me Christmas cards, and we talk on the phone occasionally."

The hurt on his face was impossible to disguise.

"I'm sorry I brought it all up," she whispered.

Grant looked at her. "No, don't apologize. It's never easy, but it's not a bad thing to talk about. Bottling it all up doesn't help. Tried it for years, and it didn't do me a bit of good. Besides, Reeve's been there for me, and I've always known he would be, no matter what."

Reeve leaned in to kiss Grant, but they were interrupted by the ding of the timer on the stove.

"Right, dinner," Reeve said, sounding amused. "Grant, why don't you finish the steaks, and we'll continue this conversation later?"

An hour later, they were seated at the table after a dinner of steak, roasted potatoes, and a salad. The leftovers were put away, the kitchen was clean, and they each had a beer—a nice Belgian ale—and Rachael knew it was time to talk about what came next.

She glanced over at Reeve, who had his foot on the rung of Grant's chair and his hand on her thigh. Grant's feet were tangled with hers under the table as he and Reeve talked. She felt the connection to both of them and felt a sense of rightness she hadn't felt with anyone before. She liked Reeve a lot. But she liked Grant too. She tried to imagine dating either one of them solo, and while it certainly wouldn't be bad, it seemed lopsided somehow. The three of them together felt just right. Balanced.

She'd had time to think. She'd spent some time with them outside of the bedroom. And she wasn't ready for this to end.

"I know you guys said I should take a few days to consider the options," she said quietly, and both Reeve and Grant turned to look at her. "But I think I've taken all the time I need. I don't know what you want, but after I talked to Jenna about it, I realized I wanted *this*." She indicated the three of them. "I want to see where this will go. I like you, Grant, and I like you, Reeve. I certainly can't imagine choosing between you."

"You don't *have* to choose," Grant said softly.

Reeve leaned forward. "You're willing to give whatever this is between us a chance? Knowing I'd like to continue to see Grant, and that we'd both like to be with you?"

"I'm willing to try," Rachael said honestly. "I have no idea if I can handle it until I try it. But I do want to find out."

"And you're okay with knowing that Grant and I would still be together, either separately or together with you?"

"Would it have to be separate?" she asked.

Reeve looked over at Grant, who shrugged and shook his head. Reeve turned back to her and ran the back of his fingers over her cheek. "Would you prefer it if Grant and I were only together when we're with you?"

She nodded but doubt assailed her. "Is that too much to ask?"

111

"I have no problem with that," Reeve replied, his tone easy and unconcerned.

God, she had no idea what she was doing. "You sure?"

"Am I sure that I could handle having a beautiful woman and a handsome man in my life?" Reeve's teeth gleamed. "Silly question."

Rachael laughed, glad she had managed to lighten such a charged conversation. "You *know* what I mean."

"I do. And I'm glad you asked, and that we're all going into this with eyes wide open, but yes, if that's what you're most comfortable with, I have no problem with it."

"I worry about causing problems between you guys, though," she admitted. "I mean, you had something way before I ever showed up. I don't want to get in the way of that …"

Grant raised his hands as if to stop her. "You're not gettin' in the way of anything. Reeve and I had three years to do our thing, and it *never* turned into a relationship. But now, I wonder if it could be different with the right woman."

"And you're suggesting that I'm the right woman?"

Grant nodded.

"Grant makes a good point." Reeve glanced over at him briefly, then looked back at her. "Maybe *this* is why it didn't happen before. Maybe Grant and I were never meant to be a couple. Maybe we were waiting for a third."

And Rachael would be their third. She could hardly believe it. She'd gone home with two guys, expecting a fun night of orgasms, and here she was a couple days later, negotiating relationship terms. It felt strangely right, though.

"Grant?" she turned to look at him, wanting to be sure he was on the same page.

He gave her a long, searching look. "I'm willing to see if we have potential as a triad. Frankly, it sounds like the sort of thing I could be very happy with."

"You said you didn't want to be monogamous."

"I wouldn't be." Grant smiled. "I'd be dating the two of you, and in the strictest sense of the word, I would definitely *not* be monogamous. But, I assume you mean would I have a problem limiting myself to two partners?"

"Yeah, basically," Rachael admitted. "I just can't imagine starting this relationship with you guys and seeing anyone else. And I think I'd drive myself crazy if you and Reeve were seeing other people too. I want this, but I want to be realistic about what I think I can handle."

Grant grabbed her hand and pressed a kiss to her palm, his stubble tickling the sensitive skin there. "Thank you for that. That's what this is going to require. All of us being honest, all the time." Rachael smiled at him. "So, I'm glad to know how you feel. As far as my ability to be faithful to just you and Grant, yes, I am willing and able, if that's what we all agree on."

Well, that was a relief. "That makes me feel better."

"Good. I do want to say one thing, though," Grant said, looking at her seriously. "Don't get so locked into what we have that you aren't willing to consider anything else. The biggest lesson I've learned is that I *never* know what life will bring me. I have surprised myself so many times with what I am interested in and capable of handling. Can you really say for sure that somewhere down the road, we won't all meet someone who we're attracted to? And that we couldn't bring them to our bed for a night and all enjoy it?"

Rachael considered the idea. "That's fair. So you're saying you want that option?"

Grant's brow furrowed for a moment. "I'm saying I want us all to remain open-minded. And be willing to have a discussion about it. I'm not saying I'll *need* someone else; I'm just saying I want us to go into this knowing that our relationship may evolve. But I will promise both of you this. I will never do anything without talking to you first. And I will never do anything that would jeopardize what we do have."

Reeve reached out and took Grant's hand. "I can agree to that."

Rachael nodded. "Me too. Although, I have no idea what I'm doing," she admitted.

"Neither do we," Reeve said. "This will be a big change for Grant and me too."

"Oh, that's reassuring," Rachael said with a laugh.

Grant chuckled. "We're not the first people to do this, Rachael. There are resources out there—books, websites, people we can talk with."

"That's true."

"Reeve and I know each other better, but we're going to have to adjust our relationship quite a bit. And you need to get to know us individually, and the three of us have to figure out how we work together. I'd be lying if I said I thought it was going to be *easy*," Grant said. His expression was earnest. "But I do think it's worth it."

"This is definitely *not* what I expected when I went into work Friday night," Rachael said ruefully.

"It's not what I expected when I showed up at your bar either," Grant admitted.

Reeve sat back and stretched. "I don't know about you two, but I'm not complaining. I had a wonderful time with you guys so far, and the future looks pretty damn good from my perspective."

Rachael smiled and stood. "I agree. Thank you."

Reeve stood as well and put his arms around her, pulling her tightly against his body for a moment. "Thank *you* for giving this a chance."

Grant stood. "Can I get in on this?"

Reeve held out an arm, and Grant slid into the spot. Reeve's arms closed around both of them, and Rachael leaned her head against Grant's shoulder. "I don't think it would be the same without you."

She could hardly believe they were both *hers*.

She had no idea what the future would hold. But it certainly wouldn't be boring with Reeve and Grant in her life.

THREE SHOTS

Brigham Vaughn

Brigham Vaughn is starting the adventure of a lifetime as a full-time writer. She devours books at an alarming rate and hasn't let her short arms and long torso stop her from doing yoga. She makes a killer key lime pie, hates green peppers, and loves wine tasting tours. A collector of vintage Nancy Drew books and green glassware, she enjoys poking around in antique shops and refinishing thrift store furniture. An avid photographer, she dreams of traveling the world and she can't wait to discover everything else life has to offer her.

Email: brighamvaughn@gmail.com
Facebook: www.facebook.com/brigham.vaughn
Facebook Author Page: www.facebook.com/pages/Author-Brigham-Vaughn/448104198635015
Facebook Fan Group (Brigham's Book Nerds):
www.facebook.com/groups/brighamsbooknerds/
Twitter: @AuthorBVaughn
G+: plus.google.com/+BrighamVaughn
Pinterest: www.pinterest.com/brighamvaughn/

Also by Brigham Vaughn

Pride Publishing (Totally Entwined Group)

Tidal Series w/ K. Evan Coles (Novels)
Wake
Calm (August 2017)

Two Peninsulas Press (Self-Published)

Standalone Short Stories
Baby, It's Cold Inside
Geeks, Nerds, and Cuddles
Love in the Produce Aisle
Not So Suddenly
Sunburns and Sunsets
The French Toast Emergencies

The Wine Tasting Series (Short Stories)
Spit or Swallow
Aftertaste
Finish

Standalone Novellas
Doc Brodie and the Big, Purple, Cat Toy

The Equals Series (Novellas)
Equals
Partners
Family (a holiday novella)

THREE SHOTS

Husbands

Connection Series (Novels)
Connection
Trust

The Midwest Series (Novels)
Bully & Exit
Push & Pull (July 2017)

Dreamspinner Press

Dr. Feelgood Anthology (Out of Print)
Pain Management